Having a boyfriend is turning my brain to mush, Gaia thought as she entered the hallway, the rose dangling by her side. It was true. She was becoming one of those shiny, happy people she so resented because she could never figure out. People like Heather and the FOHs (Friends of Heather), Megan and all the rest of them—

She froze. Thoughts of love and roses instantly vanished from her mind. A man dressed completely in black was kneeling by the door next to Sam's dorm room—picking the lock with the air of an experienced professional. Adrenaline shot through Gaia's veins. Somebody was trying to break into Sam's suite. *My boyfriend's suite.* Over her dead body. A smile crept across her face. Not only had she brought Sam a rose, she now had the opportunity to defend his honor. Luck came in strange, unforeseen ways.

Don't miss any books in this thrilling series:

FEARLESS™

Available from POCKET PULSE

FEARLESS™

TEARS

FRANCINE PASCAL

POCKET PULSE

New York   London   Toronto   Sydney   Singapore

To Burt & Jeanne Rubin

An *Original* Publication *of* POCKET BOOKS

POCKET PULSE, published by
Pocket Books, a division of Simon & Schuster, Inc.
1230 Avenue of the Americas, New York, NY 10020

Produced by 17th Street Productions,
an Alloy Online, Inc. company
33 West 17th Street
New York, NY 10011

ISBN: 0-7434-1249-4

First Pocket Pulse Paperback printing May 2001

10 9 8 7 6 5 4 3 2 1

I'm seriously considering checking myself in for a battery of psychiatric tests. I'm talking inkblots, big colored blocks, electrodes taped to my head, the works.

Ever since my father and I moved back to New York, I've been exhibiting some very strange behavior. I guess it makes sense, considering that for the first time in five years, I actually have a home. I'm no longer a stranger. I'm no longer a guest in somebody else's domain. Okay: The apartment doesn't actually belong to me or to my father. It's a two-bedroom on Mercer Street that my dad is subletting from one of his Agency friends. But that's a minor detail.

The point is, I'm part of a family who actually lives under the same roof. And yes, it's a small family. A family of two. But who cares? Size doesn't matter. I saw that in a movie poster once. So the sentiment must be true. False advertising is a major crime in this country.

Oh, yeah, that's another thing: My sense of humor is definitely suffering, too.

To complicate matters further, I've been spending a lot of time with my boyfriend, Sam Moon. There was a time (that being pretty much every waking moment until now) when the words *Gaia* and *boyfriend* would never have appeared in the same sentence unless also accompanied by words such as *joke, dream,* or *somebody else's.*

So where I once had nobody, I now have a father and a boyfriend. It's a little overwhelming, like binging on very expensive chocolate and slipping into a food coma that doesn't end but somehow is never uncomfortable. So maybe that's why my behavior has been so erratic. Here are some examples:

Exhibit A: I was shopping for dinner last week, and one of those unlistenable songs by Celine Dion or somebody was

blaring over the loudspeakers——
something about "the power of
love." And just as I reached into
the freezer for some chocolate
chocolate chip ice cream, I realized I was singing along. Right
in the middle of the frozen food
section. I didn't even realize I
knew the words. They must have
just crept into my subconscious
somehow. Anyway, needless to say,
it was a very disturbing moment.
Luckily the aisle was empty.

Exhibit B: I was headed home
along Sixth Avenue on Wednesday,
and I stopped for a second to
look at the puppies in the window
of a pet store. This isn't weird
per se. I mean, nobody is completely immune to staring at cute
puppies. I'm sure Genghis Khan
and the Marquis de Sade could
even appreciate puppies. The
weird part is that I stopped for
ten minutes. The clerk at the
store came out to ask me if
everything was all right. I'd
just been standing there, smiling

wistfully the entire time. I didn't even realize it.

Exhibit C: Sam and I were in Washington Square Park yesterday, playing chess. I don't know what came over me. The sun was setting, the slightest signs of spring were starting to show, and he was looking at me. So before I knew what was happening, we'd leaned across the chess table and *kissed*—a wet, sloppy kiss right in front of Zolov, Mr. Haq, Renny: the entire squad of my best chess-freak friends. I mean, do I even need to tell you my opinion of public displays of affection?

Three words: *Get a room*.

But there I was, smooching away as if I was an actress in a bad romance movie and the violins had just come to a huge crescendo and the camera was spinning around us endlessly, giving the audience an unfortunate case of motion sickness.

And those are just a few exam-

ples of the "new" Gaia. I'm
either in need of some drastic
and immediate psychiatric treat-
ment, or else I'm unmistakably
happy.

Happy.

There. I said the word. I didn't
throw up or have a seizure.

So maybe this is just what
happiness *is*—this kind of stupor that makes you smile at nothing, become hypnotized by
puppies, kiss in public, walk
around as if there's a sound
track behind you, belt Celine
Dion to a pint of ice cream in
aisle five, et cetera. I wouldn't
know. I haven't felt that emotion
since I was little.

Anyway, I should probably be
figuring out how and when this
whole "happy" thing is going to
fall apart. That's certainly what
the "old" Gaia would do. Be careful what you wish for, right?
That's a cliché with some truth
to it.

I don't know, though. I ask

myself: Could I just relax and appreciate this new phenomenon? Maybe there's something to be said for basking in the warm melted cheese of happiness. Maybe it's time to give five years of absolute pessimism a well-earned rest. I am, after all, the new Gaia.

Sam was utterly powerless to defend himself. Strangely, though, he felt no pain. Once **normal** **girlfriend** again, that familiar empty laughter echoed through the room. . . .

SAM'S MOUTH WAS DRY. HE TRIED

to swallow, but his lips felt as big as balloons, too thick to move.

"Cat got your tongue, boy?" a voice asked.

With his ear stuck to the cold floor, Sam couldn't move.

Ghostly Souvenirs

His entire body was strewn on its side, limp and lifeless, as a pair of dark shoes traveled in and out of his field of vision. He could barely hear the man's hollow laughter, but the footsteps on the polished wood were booming like gunfire.

I've been here before, Sam thought. *I've heard that laugh before.*

Sam's whole body was growing numb—his body, his mind. Everything was light and heavy at the same time. The voice was distant, more echo than actual sound. It was saying something about. . . Gaia.

"Do you love her, Sam?"

Sam wanted to answer. He knew the answer as instinctively as he knew his own name. But he couldn't. *Cat. . . got. . . my. . . tongue,* he thought, disoriented, trying to swallow, trying to speak. The ringing in his head was louder now, piercing his skull.

And then the door swung open. A pair of bloody sneakers marched toward Sam, nothing more than a crimson blur. Sam strained to focus on the face as the figure knelt down to him.

"Brendan?" Sam croaked.

Brendan Moss's face was covered with bruises and soaked in blood. The ringing was deafening now. His features contorted into a mask of hatred.

"You killed Mike," Brendan said, blood falling from his lips, "You tried to kill *me*, Sam." With a sharp, vicious kick Brendan lashed out at Sam's stomach. And Sam was utterly powerless to defend himself. Strangely, though, he felt no pain. Once again, that familiar empty laughter echoed through the room. . . *the laughter of that man.*

Suddenly the man came back into view, socking Brendan in the gut, sending him falling to the floor.

"No," the man said with a horrid belly laugh. He leaned down toward Sam, grabbing him by the shoulders. "We *both* tried to kill him, right, Sam? Sam?. . . Sam?"

And then Sam could see the man's face. . . the man who kept shouting his name over and over again.

"Josh?" Sam groaned, blinking.

The dream faded. The strong hands shook him mercilessly.

"Josh?" he asked again. He was no longer on the floor. He was in his bed. The remnants of sleep clung to him, but the grip was tenuous. The shaking didn't stop. Finally he snapped out of his miserable nightmare—only to find himself at the hands of his RA and new suite mate, Josh Kendall. He shoved Josh away from him almost involuntarily. "Stop it. Get off me!"

"All right! Jesus, relax," Josh said, stepping away from Sam's bed. "Calm down, man, it was just a nightmare."

Just a nightmare. Sam gaped at Josh. It had felt real, but there was nothing real about it. *And why is my skull still ringing?* Sam wondered, his throat parched. He brought a hand to his hair. He was sweating, a clammy film drenching his body as he struggled to focus his eyes on his disaster area of a dorm room. The blinking red light of his bedside clock read 5:00 A.M.

No. . . it wasn't just a dream, Sam realized. It was a flashback. It was a real memory of horror that had occurred several months earlier—when he had been kidnapped and almost died. He'd never really remembered much of what had happened. He'd spent the time in the throes of a diabetic attack, his body shutting down. Close call. For some reason, though, he'd started dreaming about it lately. He couldn't tell which parts he was making up—for instance, the part about someone asking him if he loved Gaia—and which parts were real. And that ringing—

But what was Josh doing here?

"How long have you been in my room?" Sam asked.

Josh flashed a defensive smile. "I just came in."

"But it's five in the morning," Sam croaked.

"I just thought maybe you'd answer your goddamn phone after the *twenty-fifth* ring," Josh replied, his voice teasing. He began to dig through a pile of clothing—wildly, crazily, as if he were a dog bent on retrieving a prize bone. Finally he found the phone and answered it himself. Sam hadn't even realized that the phone had been ringing the entire time.

"Hello?" Josh barked. "Hello? God*damn!*"

"Who is it?" Sam whispered, shaking his head. He was too confused and disoriented to follow what was going on.

Josh slammed the phone back into its cradle. "It was a hang-up. You must have been having some kind of nightmare. That phone rang forever."

"Oh. . . well, I'm sorry," Sam mumbled thickly. He stared at Josh, a fresh cold layer of sweat settling on his brow. Flashes of the mysterious man and blood still burned through his mind.

We both tried to kill him, right, Sam?

Somewhere in the dream logic of sleep, the image had melted from Sam's kidnapping to his recent bar brawl with Brendan, his former friend and suite mate. Somehow, three nights ago, he and Josh had ended up giving Brendan a brutal beating. True, Brendan had instigated it. True, Sam had only been defending

11

himself. But the incident had unleashed an ugly side of Sam's own personality that he'd never seen, drunk or not drunk. He just prayed he never saw it again.

But luckily (or not, depending on how one looked at it), Brendan was gone. Only three days ago he had wordlessly removed his stuff from B4 and switched to another dorm. Not that Sam could really blame him. Brendan, like the rest of NYU—not to mention NYPD detectives Reilly and Bernard—believed that Sam was responsible for Mike Suarez's death. That sad truth was that Josh was the only person who believed in Sam's innocence. And Josh was still practically a stranger.

Or was he?

Sam's eyes flashed over the guy—his chiseled jaw, his spiky black hair and sharp blue eyes, not even puffy at this hour. In some ways, Josh knew more about Sam than almost anyone... even Gaia. Sam had told him about Gaia's evil foster mother, Ella Niven, whose *Fatal Attraction*–style obsession with Sam had cost Mike his life. And put Sam firmly into prime suspect territory. But Josh had pretty much saved Sam's ass. He'd set him up with a perfect alibi to get him off the hook right before he was about to be indicted. All it took was one forged chem lab sign-in sheet, and Sam's whereabouts the night of the murder were instantly accounted for.

Sure, the sign-in sheet was fraudulent. Josh's actions might even qualify as shady. They certainly went above and beyond the obligations of a good friend—and Josh barely knew him. Moreover, Josh was also an RA, sworn to uphold the rules of the school. On one level, Sam couldn't help but think that it didn't make any sense. But maybe Josh just felt sorry for him. Whatever the reason, Sam practically owed his life to Josh. . . not to mention a debt of eternal gratitude. Without Josh's help, Sam would have been in jail at this very moment.

So why is he in my nightmares?

"Sam," Josh said sharply, snapping his fingers. "Are you gonna keep staring at me like a zombie, or do you want to get out of that bed and come with me for a run? You're freakin' me out here."

Sam swallowed, unable to answer. He lowered his eyes.

"Ease up. You're out of the woods," Josh said quietly.

Finally Sam nodded. "You're right," he whispered. The worst was over. His subconscious was just lagging behind. "Sorry. I just need to wake up. A run sounds good."

"Cool," Josh said with his usual crooked smile. "I'll catch you downstairs in five. I need to do some Achilles stretches."

"Okay."

As Josh left the suite, Sam ran a hand through his red-blond curls and forced his legs out of bed. He looked around his room in disgust. He really needed to pull his life together. How the hell would he find sweats in this mess? Towers of socks and towels greeted him from every end. The muddy carpet was hidden by a layer of Fruit Of The Loom V necks. He still hadn't brought himself to clean up since the police had turned his room into a nuclear test site. Shaking his head, he hopped up and started rummaging. A minute later he finally tracked down a pair of sweats pinned underneath a stack of library books.

A long sigh escaped his lips. He peered through his small window at the barely lit navy sky. A run did feel like a little much at this hour. But he could use it. That, and maybe a year or two holding Gaia in his arms without interruption.

He shook his head. He still couldn't fully digest that she was his girlfriend. *Gaia is my girlfriend.* The wait had been endless, intolerable. And as he pictured her thick blond hair, her powerful arms wrapped around his waist, the small of her back. . .

I want to make love to you.

The thought came to him, unbidden, seemingly out of nowhere. Not that it was unusual. He'd been having that exact thought a lot lately. They'd barely started going out, but the time was right. It would happen. But first he had to forget about the pressures of the past two weeks—

Another phone started to ring.

Sam jumped. It was coming from Josh's room, emitting a low buzz into the stillness of the suite. Sam stepped out of his room and into Josh's doorway. His pulse picked up a beat. Somebody must be calling for Mike. Maybe an old friend, somebody who didn't know he was gone. But why would they call so early? Could this be a call for Josh?

No, Josh had been using his cell phone. He'd hardly even moved into Mike's room. Some decent part of him was still no doubt waiting for Sam to give him the okay. And even though the Suarez family had come to clear everything out, a few remnants of Mike still remained. Remnants that Sam couldn't bring himself to remove. He stared at the ringing phone and the three dumbbells on the floor—ghostly souvenirs from someone who would never be back. Sam swallowed and promised that he would talk to the powers that be about having the phone number switched off that day. He took three quick steps across the room and answered it.

"Hello?" he whispered, a gnawing feeling in his gut as he held the receiver.

"Sam," a strange voice hissed. "Good morning."

"Who is this?" An arrow of fear darted up Sam's

spine. He couldn't place the voice. It was distorted. But whoever it was knew his name.

"A message from beyond." The voice chuckled, a weird crackle and fizz down the line. "Your friend Mike is worried about you. He doesn't want to see you get hurt."

Sam was wide awake now, snapped taut. Freshly rewired with fear. Someone was obviously playing some kind of sick joke. "Who the hell is this?" he spat, his knuckles white on the phone, his voice shaking.

"Do yourself a favor, Sam Moon," the voice commanded—low and threatening now, all trace of laughter gone. "Do not touch Gaia Moore. Listen to me. *Don't touch her, or you'll be sorry.*"

Sam's mind seemed to splinter into shards as he tried to process the words. Part of him wanted to hang up and run. But the caller wasn't finished.

"Don't tell anyone about this call. Especially not Gaia Moore," the voice continued. "Because if you do, your worst nightmares will come true."

A rush of blood, thick and cold, sent panic coursing through Sam's body. Was he still asleep? It was as if someone had gotten right inside his head, tunneled into his dream life. But that was. . . *impossible.*

Sam found his voice again. "Who is this?" he managed to gasp.

For a while there was silence. Then there was

another light, mirthless chuckle—more like water running through a drain than any human sound.

"Who is this?" Sam repeated, more urgently.

"I'm watching you, Sam."

The line went dead.

"ARE YOU SURE YOU'RE PUTTING

Some Male Territorial Thing

enough of that in the filter?" Gaia joked as Sam tipped half a pack of coffee into the coffeemaker.

"If it isn't strong, then it's not coffee," Sam muttered. His hands seemed unusually clumsy as he dropped mounds of brown coffee grains all over the kitchen table. He was jumpy. Then again, he'd probably already had a few cups of coffee already. "It should be somewhere between liquid and the consistency of wet tar," he joked, but his voice was brittle.

Gaia wrinkled her nose, staring at him, trying to figure out what was on his mind. Then she shrugged and offered her mug. If Sam liked his coffee to taste like sludge, that was fine with her. Because she was here. She was with him—having breakfast with him at 7:45 A.M. on a Monday in his dorm. Just like a normal girlfriend. All in all, it was a good start to the morning. Coffee, doughnuts, and Sam: the only valid reasons to get up on a day she'd otherwise consider a write-off and maybe dodge in favor of scamming Zolov at the chess tables in Washington Square Park.

Gaia took a sip, then made a face. "Mmmm. Motor oil," she teased.

But Sam didn't seem to hear her. He sipped from his own mug and stared out the window with a vacant gaze.

All right. Something was definitely going on here. She put down her mug and moved over to Sam, then wrapped her arms around his waist and met his gaze. For a moment they just stood there. Gaia allowed her eyes to soak in every aspect of Sam's face: the pensive mouth, the curls that seemed to change color depending on the light—but most of all, those amazing hazel eyes. . . the patterns in the irises like shattered glass. Or gold spiderwebs. Gaia felt her pulse quicken, her stomach flip and jangle. But Sam seemed stuck in some kind of temporary cryofreeze.

"Hello?" she whispered.

Still no response.

Gaia's brow furrowed, silently pressing him for an

answer, but this only made him look away. Her pulse slowed. She stepped back. Clearly this was not the time to make an attempt at a romantic moment or even to ask what was wrong. She didn't understand it. Sam had been like a manic-depressive ever since she'd gotten back from France—reeling from bouts of extreme highs one moment and grimly tense the next. At first she'd thought it was just the roller-coaster strangeness and freshness of their relationship. Of course, there was also the small fact that she'd taken off for Europe with her supposedly sick uncle—only to have returned with her father and discovered that Uncle Oliver was a psycho terrorist. It was a hell of a lot for Gaia to knock back, and maybe more for Sam.

All at once she felt guilty. Maybe Sam was just plain old freaked out. Did he even know what he'd been getting himself into by diving into this fledgling relationship with the daughter of a CIA agent? It wasn't exactly par for the course for a well-adjusted premed. Not to mention the small fact that Gaia hadn't exactly managed to tell Sam what was happening during these European high-jinks escapades. She'd e-mailed, but his computer had been taken in for repairs. Sam had been near frantic when she got back. She'd all but disappeared.

But we're cool now, she said to herself. *Or on our way to being cool. At least we're cooler than we were when I always found myself bursting in on him and Heather. . . .*

19

She exhaled slowly. Maybe it was nothing. For all she knew, Sam just wasn't a morning person. But somehow Gaia doubted that one.

Most likely it was still Mike.

Gaia hadn't really known Mike Suarez, but Sam had been devastated when he OD'd. He refused to talk about it. Gaia knew that feeling only too well. All the Oprahs in the world could glibly expound on your indisputable need to "share" when you were "hurting."

But not everyone was the same. Grief did strange things to people.

"Are you okay?" Gaia finally asked, searching Sam's troubled eyes. "You're thinking about Mike, aren't you?"

Sam shook his head almost violently. Without a word he brought his mug to the sink, dumping out the fresh cup he'd just poured himself. "I'm fine," he said as he rinsed it out about six times. He turned back to Gaia. "It's just. . . I have a lot of work and stuff. I've sort of fallen behind."

"Hmmm," Gaia murmured doubtfully. But she didn't press it. Instead she just walked over and took his hand. Her finger brushed over the artery in his wrist.

Holy shit. His pulse was racing. Her eyes narrowed in concern. "Jesus, there's a techno rave going on inside your body," she murmured.

"I'm *fine,*" Sam insisted with a faint smile, pulling his wrist away and putting his arms around her.

Yes, definitely best not to press it. Sam would share

when he was ready. "Hey. . . is your computer back yet?" Gaia asked, trying to change the subject to something lighter. "You know, I sent you something from Paris." She blushed slightly. "An e-mail. I guess you could say it was kind of a confession." *More like a love letter,* she added silently, although the message was clearly implied.

"No, uh, it's still in the shop," Sam answered. His tone was odd, formal.

Gaia arched an eyebrow. Cagey again. Nothing Sam said was sounding right. But he suddenly turned and leaned down, planting his lips on her own. And in that moment she felt like she had been transported back to singing in that ice-cream aisle; the kiss washed away all the worries and doubts—

A phone rang in another room. The shrill buzz cut through the sweet silence.

Gaia felt Sam's back stiffen as he jerked away from her. He stood stock still for two more rings. Then he shook his head. "You know what?" he muttered, dragging her out of the kitchen. "Let's get out of here."

"You're not going to answer it?" Gaia asked as she let Sam pull her to the door.

"The machine can get it," he mumbled. He threw on his coat and tossed Gaia her own worn leather jacket. "Come on, I'll walk you to school."

Gaia had to smile. "Chivalry? I thought you had to study."

"Lots of wackos out there." Sam flashed her a quick

grin. They took the stairs down to street level and exited the glass doors of 32 Fifth Avenue. He was joking, obviously. If there was one thing Gaia could do, it was take care of herself. In fact, deleting wackos from the NYU district was about as close to a daily cleansing regimen as Gaia would ever have. But less than a minute later Sam was unsmiling and serious again. He took her hand, his eyes flicking left and right as they headed toward the miniature Arc de Triomphe in Washington Square Park. The crisp, late winter air sent a brief shiver down Gaia's back.

"Game after school?" she asked, looking in the direction of the chess tables, empty of regulars at this time in the morning.

"Maybe, yeah," Sam replied. He surveyed the park.

"Maybe?" Gaia echoed.

"I mean, yes," Sam said, flashing her a brief but genuine smile. He kissed her on the cheek. She couldn't help but notice that the skin on his face seemed taut. Dark circles lined the wells of his eyes. He turned away. "Oh, you know what? I forgot. I can't walk you to school. I have an exam this morning. . . . I'll see you later, all right?"

Gaia gaped at him as he turned and hurried back up Fifth Avenue.

Her face hardened. Whatever. That wasn't just rude; it was *harsh*. And completely un-Sam-like. But if he wanted to act like a freak, fine. She whirled and marched through Washington Square West, her sneakers clomping on the pavement. Her thoughts raced. She was angry, yes. But still, she knew deep down that the anger would be short-lived. His tenseness could mean a whole number of things. His flailing former 4.0 GPA. The forty bucks he'd lost to her playing chess the day before. This exam that he had to take.

A fleeting smile crossed her face. Maybe this was just what having a boyfriend was like. How would she know? Gaia had never had a boyfriend before. Maybe boyfriends got all preoccupied and mood swingy once they'd won you over—once you got comfy in their sock-smelling bedroom. Maybe it was some male-territorial thing.

Gaia's smile widened. Here she was, running to make it to school on time. Worrying about her boyfriend's mood.

So close to normal, it was freaky.

PAY ATTENTION, ED.

An Invisible Band-Aid

Ed Fargo had to keep reminding himself to listen to Gaia as they headed down the hallway at school. It wasn't that he didn't want to listen. But ever since his operation—the operation that could very well bring back full use of his legs—Ed had replaced all his world-class listening skills with total self-involvement. And this was a quality Ed happened to despise more than most. Here was Gaia, finally back from Paris and back in his life, their friendship totally back on track. . . and what was Ed thinking about? Himself. Just as he had been for weeks.

He couldn't help it, though. He wasn't staying positive like Dr. Feldman had told him. But how much longer could he keep this operation a goddamn secret? *You're doing it again,* Ed scolded himself. *It's Gaia, for God's sake. Pay attention.* He desperately tried to focus again on Gaia as they headed for MacGregor's English class. His grip tightened on his wheels. The only problem was, even when he tried to listen, he had no idea what the hell Gaia was talking about.

"Reality TV." Gaia snorted as she heaved her messenger bag over her broad, perfectly sculpted shoulder. "I can't believe all these people tune in for something that's even more boring than their real lives."

"Hmmm," Ed grunted, trying to keep up with Gaia's massive strides and her uncharacteristically happy, free-floating monologue on bad TV. His wheelchair squeaked on the linoleum.

"Stuck in a house for a whole month with only one tube of lipstick," Gaia mocked, mimicking an announcer's overearnest voice. "How will they. . . *survive?*"

But Ed could barely simulate even the dim cousin of a smile. He couldn't stay tuned. He was on a completely different channel. *I'm sick of this chair. When I get out of this thing, I'm inviting everyone to a party under the Brooklyn Bridge, and we're going to burn this thing. . . if I ever get the chance to tell anyone.* His lips tightened.

He tried not to think about his deal with Heather. It seemed like he was *always* trying not to think about his deal with Heather. He'd promised her that he wouldn't tell a soul, not even Brian, his physical therapist, about any potential progress he made with his legs. That way he could still cash in on the settlement. That way he could still help Heather, whose family was fast going broke. Twenty-six million dollars would solve everyone's problems—

So why did he feel like shit?

Actually, he knew the answer. He knew the answer because he was making progress. The physical therapy was working. He'd been busting his ass like an Olympic athlete in training, and it was starting to pay off. Pins and needles in his left quad. A twitch in four of his toes. All he wanted to do was tell Gaia. But he'd sworn himself to secrecy. To Heather.

Ed felt wrong about it on so many levels, but he'd agreed. Stupid? Probably. But he hadn't been able to say no to Heather. Not after everything they'd been through—not when he could save her entire family

25

from their financial crisis. He knew it was for a good cause, but all the secrets and lies were just closing him off from everyone. And that was the last thing he needed.

"You find me fascinating, don't you, Fargo?" Gaia came to a sudden halt in the hallway, crossed her arms, and stared Ed down, missing nothing, as per usual.

And also, as per usual, Ed once again found himself amazed at how stunningly gorgeous she was. Of course, she was checking him out as if he'd just offered her a turd sandwich. Not that he could blame her. She'd been talking up a storm, and he'd given exactly one grunt the entire time.

"What's with you?" she asked.

Ed opened his mouth, then closed it. He didn't trust himself, knowing only too well that the secret might just fly out of him if he wasn't damned careful. He hated keeping things from Gaia. Especially after they'd recently gone through a bad hump and only just revived their friendship.

"Seriously, Fargo, have you found the Lord or what? Your eyes are all glinty, and your lip is zipped. Give it up."

"It's, well. . ." Ed swallowed. "It's. . . things are good with Heather is all. And I know you don't want to hear about that." A sinking feeling swept over him as annoyance flitted across Gaia's face. He was lying, for one thing. Things were not good with Heather. But more important, the *H* word was best not passed between him and Gaia. It was an unspoken agreement. An invisible Band-Aid necessary to hold their friendship together. And now he'd gone and verbalized them into awkwardness.

On the other hand, what else could he have said?

You could tell the truth, he hollered at himself, dying to get it out of his system.

But that would only make it worse. Then he'd have to explain how it needed to be a secret. How Heather needed the insurance money to help get her family out of debt. Thereby giving Gaia yet another reason to hate Heather. It was an extraordinarily vicious circle. And Ed was right in the middle of it, swirling like toilet water.

"We better get in there," Gaia said evenly, looking toward the classroom as Mr. MacGregor walked through the door. "Or maybe I'll go ahead by myself," she amended coolly, turning to look over Ed's shoulder.

Ed spun and followed her gaze. Heather. Of course. Ed watched as Heather came closer, materializing out of the shadowy corridor like a walking Maybelline commercial. *My girlfriend,* he thought. She was beautiful, no doubt: that long brown hair, that perfect figure. But as she walked toward him, her smile broadening even in spite of Gaia's presence, Ed felt his spirits sink. Why did the two best things in his life—Heather and the fact that he might be able to walk again—feel more like curses than blessings?

Actually, it was best not to think too hard about that. It was best not to think too hard about anything right now.

Ed,
    Suggestion:
    Who? You and me.
    Where? My house.
    When? Tonight.
    What? "Watching videos." (Note use of quotation
marks.)
    So what do you say?
                            Love,
                            Heather
P.S. Careful passing this. I think MacGregor's on to me.

Heather,
    Sorry, I can't. Too much homework.
    Talk later,
                            Ed

The fragile house of cards he'd built to protect himself was beginning to **unshaven** crumble. The voice **ghost** on the phone echoed through his head. *Your worst nightmares will come true. . . .*

"MOON, YOU LOOK LIKE CRAP," Josh remarked, giving Sam a sharp once-over.

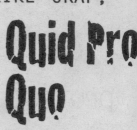

Quid Pro Quo

"I feel like crap," Sam concurred. He tried to ignore Josh as he took a gulp of his water and scanned the street through the window of Eddie's Diner. He rubbed his hands over the stubble on his face, then downed the rest of the glass. He was thirsty. Tired. His throat felt raw and tight. He grimaced as he caught his reflection in the mirror on the opposite wall. Josh was right. Sam was an unshaven ghost.

Josh chuckled. "Enough already with the whole homeless look," he muttered. He grabbed a fistful of Sam's fries and scarfed them down as he spoke. "When are you going to clean up and *wake* up? You're free and clear. The situation with the cops is watertight. *You're no longer a suspect.*"

Sam suddenly found himself examining Josh again, the same way he had that morning in his bedroom. There was such confidence in his voice, such assurance.

"How do you *know* that?" Sam asked finally. "How do you always *know* my status with the police?"

"I know a few people," Josh replied with an easy shrug.

Sam kept staring.

Josh caught his eyes. "Why, do you think I'm a cop?" He laughed once.

"I just. . . forget it," Sam mumbled, shaking his head slowly. He didn't know what he thought anymore. Maybe people never really knew who their friends were. Maybe it was just something one couldn't know. After all, Sam had thought Brendan was a trusted friend, and he saw how that had turned out. He stared down at his untouched burger. "I just don't think I'm out of the woods. There've been some other things going on. . . ."

That ugly whisper began to haunt Sam again.

Don't touch her, or you'll be sorry.

"Things? What things?" Josh's eyes narrowed. He looked at Sam as if he were on drugs.

"Never mind," Sam whispered, checking the street again. He didn't even know what he was looking for—*who* he was looking for. What did the enemy look like?

I'm watching you, Sam.

"Hey, Sammy, you're scaring me here—"

"Can you do me a favor?" Sam interrupted, flashing back to the morning's nightmare. "Can you *not* call me 'Sammy'? I can't stand it. It just. . . it really rubs me the wrong way. I'm sorry. I just don't like it."

Josh gave Sam a long stare. Sam couldn't read it at all. He'd recently started to notice that Josh had the ultimate poker face. There could have been anything behind his stare: hurt, anger, confusion. There could have been nothing at all. But Sam made no effort to avert his glance. For a moment they were immersed in an impromptu staring contest. Until the bright smile returned to Josh's face.

"No problem," Josh said. Then he shook his head and sighed to himself. "Man, I create the perfect alibi for you, and this is what I get in return. 'Don't call me Sammy.' Way to be a pal, Sammy—sorry—*Sam*."

Guilt and self-loathing squirmed unpleasantly in Sam's gut. He should have kept his mouth shut. Josh could call him whatever he wanted. Josh had saved him from a life in prison, regardless of the fact that his methods were questionable. Anyway, it wasn't Josh's fault that he was starring in Sam's nightmares. Nor was it Josh's fault that someone was trying to drive Sam to the brink of insanity with harassing telephone calls. Sam straightened and took a deep breath. He needed to adjust his attitude if he was going to stay sane.

"I'm sorry," he announced. "You're right. I'm free and clear, and I need to start enjoying it." Maybe all this other stuff was in Sam's head. A couple of bad dreams and some asshole prank caller. "And I owe it to *you*, Josh. I owe you big time."

For a moment Josh stared at him again. Then he flashed that inscrutable smile. "Do you mean that?" he asked.

"Of course," Sam replied.

"Good." With a satisfied nod Josh reached down to his messenger bag on the floor, then pulled out a brown paper-wrapped package. "Because now that you mention it, there *is* something you could do for me."

Sam hesitated, his eyes narrowing. That was a little convenient, wasn't it? Had Josh been waiting this whole time for an opportune moment to ask for a favor? But then Sam shook his head. Even if Josh *had* been simply fishing for a favor, he had earned the right to do whatever he wanted.

"You've got it," Sam said.

Josh pushed the package over to Sam's side of the table.

"I need you to take this package to this address after we're done here," Josh stated. His tone became oddly businesslike. "It's in TriBeCa. The place will look abandoned. It's kind of an old warehouse, but don't worry. Follow the instructions, and someone will be there for the pickup." With that, Josh went right back to his meal.

Again Sam hesitated, waiting for a further explanation. None came. He stared at the package. An address on White Street. No name on it.

"What is it?" Sam asked.

"Don't worry about it," Josh replied, munching away on his burger.

Sam's head jerked up at the sudden sharpness in Josh's voice. He had no idea how to respond. He just sat there, baffled. What was going on here? A bizarrely succinct list of instructions, a brown paper package, an abandoned warehouse. . . none of it exactly filled him with a sense of well-being. A slew of unfortunate scenarios ran through his head. He tried to ignore all of them. Only a few seconds ago he'd decided to stop being so paranoid. But there was no way he was going to deliver that package. He didn't know what was in it, and he didn't really care. He considered all his options and decided to go with the simplest choice.

"I can't," Sam said finally, searching Josh's eyes for a reaction. As per usual, there was no visible change. "I've got an organic chem seminar all day."

"You can skip the seminar," Josh said, finishing off his burger. It wasn't as if he was making a suggestion; it was as if he was issuing a command.

Sam frowned. "No, I can't."

"Well, that doesn't seem fair, does it?" Josh asked with a laugh.

"Fair?"

"You say you'll do me this favor." His smile instantly vanished. "I ask you to do it. And then you take it back. That makes you a hypocrite, Sam."

Sam's eyes bulged. He couldn't believe what he was hearing. "But I—"

"You know what an Indian giver is, Sam?" Josh interrupted.

"A . . . *what?*" Sam shook his head. His jaw hung slack. He hadn't heard that term in ten years. Not only was it offensive, it was childish. Coming from Josh. . .

"When someone gives you something and then takes it back?" Josh pressed.

"Yeah, I know what it means," Sam muttered slowly.

Josh raised his eyebrows. "You offered a favor, and then you took it back. That would be like me giving you that alibi and then taking it back."

Sam flinched. "I—I—"

"No, really," Josh interrupted again. "I mean, how would you like it if I did that? You wouldn't like that, would you? If I went back to the cops and told them your alibi was a fake? I mean, that wouldn't be very nice, would it? That would make me an Indian giver. That would put you in shit twice as deep! How much would *that* suck?" Josh shook his head with another hollow laugh.

The unpleasant feeling in Sam's gut seemed to expand, like a balloon. This conversation suddenly felt very surreal. He couldn't tell if Josh was joking or not. But what he was saying was absolutely true. At least before the fake alibi, Sam was truly innocent, whether people believed him or not. But once Josh got Sam to sign that forged sign-in sheet, Sam had officially become a criminal—guilty of fraud and perjury. And if Josh ever told the cops about it, Sam would then look guilty of the murder. Why would someone lie to cover a crime they didn't commit?

"Relax, man," Josh assured him. "I'm just making a point here, that's all. Don't freak out on me." He turned to the waitress at the counter. "Can we get a check here?"

Sam started shaking his head, his heart racing. "Wait," he said softly as the waitress slapped the check on their table. "I'm just not. . . are you saying. . . I mean, what—what are you saying here?"

"Relax," Josh repeated, smiling again and looking Sam in the eye. "If you do this favor for me. . . then I'm not saying anything, right? So just do it, and everything will be fine." He shrugged. "It doesn't take a premed at NYU to figure that one out, Sammy."

Sam couldn't speak. He was speechless as he stared at Josh's smiling face. Speechless and more than a little scared. There was no use fighting paranoia anymore because now Sam knew that he had every reason to be paranoid. The fragile house of cards he'd built to protect himself was beginning to crumble. The voice on the phone echoed through his head. *Your worst nightmares will come true. . . .*

Josh dropped a twenty down on the table and slid the package into Sam's lap. "Thanks for the favor, dude," he said casually. He pulled on his coat and headed toward the door. "I might need a couple more deliveries after this one. But just remember, we're in this together, Sammy—oh, shit, sorry—*Sam.*" He paused and frowned. "Actually, you know what? I think I'm just going to call you Sammy. I like the sound of it better."

And then he was gone.

Whacked-Out Impulse

"OH, CEENDY." ZOLOV SIGHED, TAP-ping the head of his red Mighty Morphin Power Ranger on the table next to him. He stared at the chessboard.

Gaia had to smile. Zolov had never called her anything other than Cindy—even after all these months, even after she'd saved his life. But then, she supposed it was hard to break any ninety-year-old man of his habits, particularly one who didn't speak English very well.

"Even he is shocked," Zolov went on, pointing to his cherished action figure with an ancient, gnarled hand. "You leave yourself wide open for the bishop. Thees ees a move of a *complete* amateur. You are better than this, Ceendy."

What? Dumbfounded, Gaia's eyes mapped the

board in one quick, mathematically precise second. Her smile turned to a smirk. Zolov was right. She couldn't believe she'd opened herself up for checkmate so early on in a game. It was a rookie mistake.

"Jesus." Shaking her head, Gaia slapped down a twenty-dollar bill. "I nailed myself."

Zolov swiftly pocketed the cash. No mercy at their table.

"It is love," he joked, his tiny, raisin-black eyes twinkling. From him, the word *love* sounded more like *loaf*. "You can't play anymore. No more fire. All thoughts on boyfriend."

Gaia rolled her eyes, but she blushed slightly, too. Once again Zolov was dead-on. Her chess game had suffered immeasurably ever since she and Sam had gotten together. You couldn't think about your boyfriend and play with a grand master.

"Where is Sam?" Zolov asked, shielding his eyes from the sun as he surveyed the park. "You have date, no?"

Gaia nodded absently. Sam had agreed to meet her for chess in the park. He was now officially a half hour late. They had barely started dating, and he was already standing her up? Part of her felt obliged to be severely pissed. But the other part was doing her damnedest not to take it personally. Sam hadn't been himself this morning. Had he run into some kind of problem? Had that exam taken longer than expected? Maybe Mike's death wasn't

40

the only thing upsetting Sam. He'd said he had a lot of studying. Maybe he was just working in his room and he'd lost track of time. . . .

She nodded to herself. She should give him the benefit of the doubt.

And at that moment, for some reason, a completely inane thought popped into her head.

Bring him a rose.

Gaia had no clue where this thought had come from. She couldn't *see* any roses; all she saw were the lifeless trees and frostbitten grass of the park. And since when did standing up a girlfriend earn a guy a gift? Actually, the real question was this: Since when did Gaia think of bringing *anyone* a rose? What was this, 1955? Pretty soon she'd be bouncing around in poodle skirts and asking Sam to the sock hop.

She remembered what Ed had asked her, not too long ago, when their relationship had been at an all-time low: *"Who are you, and what have you done with Gaia Moore?"*

Recently, it seemed, she had no idea. The old Gaia Moore was nothing more than a memory at times.

"You go to Sam now, Ceendy," Zolov said, as if reading her thoughts.

She nodded, distracted, then flashed him a quick smile and waved as she hurried out of the park. She headed straight for the Korean deli on the corner of Sam's block. Maybe this was a completely

41

whacked-out impulse, but she would run with it. Why not? Sam would appreciate its unexpectedness. It might even help to crack his shell, to get him to confide in her. Besides, a single rose only cost two bucks. She paid for it quickly and ran the rest of the way to Sam's dorm. With a perfunctory wave at the bloated security guard (he and Gaia were all but on a first-name basis at this point), she dashed up the stairwell. It was odd, but she was worried if she slowed down, she might begin to have doubts—and then she wouldn't give him the rose at all.

Having a boyfriend is turning my brain to mush, she thought as she entered the hallway, the rose dangling by her side. It was true. She was becoming one of those shiny, happy people she so resented because she could never figure them out. People like Heather and the FOHs (Friends of Heather), Megan and all the rest of them—

She froze. Thoughts of love and roses instantly vanished from her mind. A man dressed completely in black was kneeling by the door next to Sam's dorm room—picking the lock with the air of an experienced professional. Adrenaline shot through Gaia's veins. Somebody was trying to break into Sam's suite. *My boyfriend's suite.* Over her dead body. A smile crept across her face. Not only had she brought Sam a rose, she now had the opportunity to defend his honor. Luck came in strange, unforeseen ways.

"Hey!" she shouted, building up speed.

The black-clad figure reacted like a fleeting apparition. Instead of rising to challenge her, he simply dropped the lock pick in a black leather bag, then snatched it up and moved swiftly toward the stairs on the opposite side of the hall. He didn't bother to look behind him.

"Hey!" Gaia hollered again.

He broke into a run. A second later he crashed through the stairwell door and disappeared from sight. Gaia scowled. Now she was mad. Energy crackled like electricity in her body. No way was she going to let this scumbag get away. She threw Sam's rose to the ground and pumped her legs like a racehorse, exploding through the door before it had even closed behind the guy, then jumping the first flight of steps in one leap—

Thwip. Thwip.

Gaia knew the sound instinctively: gunfire. She reacted before she even knew what she was doing, ducking behind the banister. The man in black had pulled out a nine millimeter with a silencer and fired off two quick shots. Two crackling holes blew open in the cinder block wall directly behind her.

Her adrenaline was at a fever pitch. It was a good thing she could feel no fear. She didn't exactly have the advantage in this situation. A gun had been completely unexpected. But rage clouded her judgment. She could

43

have let the guy go as he galloped down the stairs, but instead she vaulted over the banister like a gymnast. In a swift maneuver she slid down the next floor's banister, building up an enormous amount of momentum.

The man was right in front of her now. She targeted his head—sliding off the metal and snapping out her leg for a perfectly placed side kick.

"Hai!"

His mouth dropped open a fraction of a second before the toe struck—and his head slammed into the wall. An instant later he and everything he had with him went tumbling down the last of the stairs. A small black wire fell from his bag as he hit the bottom landing. Gaia sucked in her breath as she landed, throwing her arms wide to gain her balance.

There was a moment of quiet. Gaia peered at the untidy black heap below her. The man was unconscious.

Or so she thought.

Dizziness began to claw at her brain. She grabbed the banister for support.

Without warning, the man grabbed the gun and his bag and vanished into the lobby. He left the mysterious black wire behind. Gaia simply watched him go. Battle fatigue was beginning to kick in: that inevitable physical aftermath. Aside from fearlessness, it was the only part of Gaia's singular physical chemistry that she did not understand.

Why did she always pass out after a fight, as if her nearly superhuman abilities were on some kind of timer? But she knew she wouldn't answer that question now. She summoned up the strength to grab the wire from the floor, then made her way back to Sam's door. Purple dots swam before her eyes as she scooped up Sam's rose and pounded on his door.

"Sam?" she called, gasping for breath. She tried to examine the black wire. Her face twisted in a grimace. There was a tiny silver microphone at one end. So, from what she could tell, it was a cutting-edge piece of surveillance equipment. Definitely expensive. Something her father might have. But why the hell would somebody try to install that in Sam's suite?

Gaia pounded on the door once more.

"Sam?" she hollered. The hall began to spin around her. The rose slipped from her fingers, and then she slipped after it into a well of blackness.

What an extraordinary gift it is for me to experience the ordinary.

For years I've had to live a life that any ordinary, sane person would call madness. Terrorists. Aliases. Living in hiding. I've seen every kind of horror and injustice. I've seen the worst kind of depravity inflicted on innocent victims. I wonder sometimes how I've managed to keep my own sanity through all these years. I watched my brother surrender to some kind of madness.

A madness that took my Katia from me. A madness that still threatens every moment to take Gaia from me as well.

I wonder what my sick brother is thinking at this very moment, surrounded by gray prison walls. I know he is seething. I know he must be drowning in his own spite—his own desperate need for vengeance. And knowing that fills me with sadness. Not just for him, but because I know these beautifully ordinary days with

Gaia can only last so long. So I am savoring every moment.

Tonight I made a leg of lamb for dinner while my daughter set the table and complained about her boyfriend. At dinner I listened to her grumbling about his missing an after-school date. And then after dinner I did the dishes as she read the newspaper. I demanded that she do her homework beforehand, and she argued—rightly—that she didn't need to study for her French test. But I argued back just the same. Though my daughter is a gifted linguist, I thought for once I would try to just be a dad, like a million other dads at that moment all around the city.

To anyone else, this would be just another ordinary evening. But to me it was anything but. To me it was unforgettable.

I pray that days like these won't end. I wish every new day could be as perfectly banal.

But I know my twin brother.

It is hard for me to fathom my reversal of fortune. So close to having Gaia. My Gaia. The daughter that should have been mine. But now, according to the latest missive received from J, my precious girl is living with Tom. It makes my flesh crawl.

I must be patient. I envision her angelic face, so reminiscent of Katia's—yet also a face that carries my strength, my will.

My DNA.

Yes, every time I see my own image in her, I am blessed. It is like reading a tiny love letter from Katia to me, every time.

Except that now she is looking at Tom. Living with Tom. Letting him guide her, take her farther and farther away from me.

I am the only man who truly loves her, who truly understands what she was born to be.

I must be patient.

It is only a matter of time before I will be out of this prison, away from the uncouth company of petty killers and common thugs, from this vulgar zoo of lowest-common-denominator behavior. I must constantly remind myself that there is humor to be found in the situation. After all, this is the Manhattan federal jail—the facility where the world's most dangerous men are routinely held captive. The World Trade Center bombers were quarantined here. And yet the security is so extraordinarily lax.

Of course, for most prisoners the security must seem quite threatening indeed. Armed guards in every corridor and at every exit at all times. Infrared cameras, ten-inch-thick steel doors. But for me these factors merely represent an occasional hindrance. My body is trapped, but my thoughts are free to roam. As are my commands. Visitors can still get inside the front door, and that is all I need. The sad fact of the matter is that the line between criminal and guard is an

imaginary one at best—easily
blurred or erased with a bribe.

To say that all criminals are
the same is to stereotype in the
most base and ignorant fashion.
There is no one here like me. How
I loathe these plebeian crooks!
Their aspirations in life are so
ultimately unimportant. They con-
stitute no noble ambition or pure
design. For the most part they
are driven by greed: for money,
for power, for sex. They can't
see past it.

My patience is wearing thin.

But the world will change. I
know it. I must concentrate my
energies on the moment when I
shall be free to reclaim what is
mine. What should have been mine
all along. Like Katia herself.

Katia. Her death was a mistake. My only regret. Her lovely
eyes stare back at me in my
dreams, dead and vacant. Blood in
her magnificent hair. She haunts
me, my one regret, the sweetest
of loves.

But one regret focuses a man's will. Deepens his convictions. Forces him to confront himself. Spurs him on to attain his goals and master his own hubris. This introspection is a test of courage. To regret is to acknowledge one's humanity and weakness. That is the first step toward strength. Yes, one regret is of utmost importance. But two regrets would merely amount to failure. And I do not intend to fail. I shall escape this meaningless purgatory of prison. My brother will pay for putting me here. And Gaia will soon be mine.

This time forever.

it was whatever came in a close second to fear: some nerve-splaying, bone-charging kind of anticipation that **lightning** felt crazy and sane all at the same time.

"SO I'M, LIKE, THINKING THIS

Potential Pouffing— Out Factor

place will give me the killer haircut of my life." Megan Stein moaned as Heather and her friends stepped into the lunch line. "But I go home looking like a hair commercial, and I wake up looking like a blond Ronald McDonald." Megan glanced behind her, her eyes wide in a very obvious plea for a pat on the back.

"You *so* do *not* look like a blond Ronald McDonald," Tina Lynch soothed, right on cue. "You so do not."

"Heather, what do you think?" Megan whined, her hand flying up again to smooth down (and show off) her newly and expensively coifed hair. "I am *so* completely dying over this cut!"

What a tragedy, Heather thought, keeping her sarcasm silent. She knew the deal. Oh, yes. Now she had to compliment Megan. She had to tell Megan that not only did she *not* resemble the blond Ronald McDonald, not even faintly; moreover, she looked incredible. Like a supermodel. The sad thing was, the old Heather would have no problem with this. This ritual of fishing for compliments, this routine of affirmation, was so tightly woven into the fabric of their lives that none of them even noticed it anymore. Every single one of her friends, especially Megan, always turned to her, Heather, for a pat on the back.

But Heather had bigger things to worry about than the potential pouffing-out factor of Megan's new hairdo. She could only mumble the faintest grunt of a wishy-washy "you-look-great" before picking out a chicken sandwich. She bit her lip, momentarily tasting her Kiehl's peppermint lip balm. Which, come to think of it, was yet another thing she'd have to ration. Because she could no longer afford even that most minor of luxuries.

"I look so fat with this cut." Megan groaned, apparently not picking up on Heather's lack of enthusiasm—or maybe trying desperately to get Heather to commiserate. "Can someone please tell me why this cafeteria insists on supplying us with only the most fattening foods?"

"So disgusting," Tina agreed, averting her eyes from a dish of mashed potatoes. "I mean, look at all that starch! Clearly they cater only to the Amazonians of this world, like Gaia Moore. Or else to the bulimics."

All the girls sniggered together.

Except Heather. She was horrified. The pit of her stomach hardened. Jokes about bulimics weren't exactly a laugh a minute right now. Not since her sister, Phoebe, had been hospitalized for full-fledged anorexia and was evidently not getting any better—even though Heather's unemployed father had bankrupted the Gannis family on the most expensive care Manhattan could offer. Heather turned to her friends, hurt clouding her eyes. And then she remembered why they were being so insensitive. They had no idea about Phoebe. Or her parents' bankruptcy. Or anything else that mattered to her.

Only Ed knew. And only Ed cared.

Scanning over the top of Megan's perfectly shagged new head, Heather searched the cafeteria for Ed. Yes, they were going through a rough patch, but Heather needed to be with him right now. She needed to feel like she actually existed as a human being, not just a style barometer. *At least fighting reminds you that you're human,* she thought wistfully, recalling the recent misunderstandings and tensions. But maybe this time, at lunch, she and Ed could just talk, be together. They could just eat the goddamned starchy mashed potatoes—

That was when she spotted him. At the far corner table. With Gaia.

Instantly Heather's heart squeezed. Her blood felt like it was turning to ice. What the hell was Gaia even *doing* here, anyway? Wasn't she supposed to be off in Europe or something? Maybe Ed's weirdness didn't have to do with their little bargain. Ed had blown her off yesterday on the phone; he'd stiffed her earlier today. Maybe this was about Gaia.

Every time Gaia Moore turned up in Heather's world, she ruined everything. With her Greek goddess name and looks, she caused trouble everywhere she went. *They should have named her Nemesis,* Heather thought miserably, following Tina, Megan, and the others to a table. *That's Greek, isn't it?* A hollow laugh escaped her lips. The knot in her stomach disentangled and then re-formed, harder than before. Heather felt like she'd swallowed a crystal. Or a splinter of glass. Unconsciously her eyes wandered back to Ed and Gaia.

There's no way Ed would tell Gaia about what he agreed to do for me, is there?

No. Of course not. Ed loved her. And she loved him. She had no doubts about that. They trusted each other. But still, deep down, she knew she was compromising that love and trust by asking him to hang on to his settlement—to discourage anyone from thinking he would walk again so as to help Heather's family financially.

She was barely conscious of slumping down between Megan and Tina. At least they were being polite to her. That was something. Recently they'd treated her like dirt. They'd drop her in a second if they knew she was broke, too. God, it was an awful mixture, love and money. Heather didn't have a choice not to take this path. She had to help her family. Even if it meant risking her relationship with Ed.

Because if she didn't help them, who would?

"OH, GOD, GAIA," SAM MURMURED, wrapping Gaia tightly in his arms. "I'm so sorry. I'm so, so sorry...."

Soap Opera Cliché

Gaia found herself surrendering to his embrace. It was so strange: She was fearless, powerful, strong, a fighter. But in Sam's presence she was powerless to resist a simple hug. She'd walked into this dorm room with every intention of scolding him for their missed date. She had planned to let him have it—to tell him about her whole encounter with the burglar, about waking up alone in his hall and staggering home, about buying the rose and throwing it away... but the moment Sam had seen her, he'd apologized profusely and then begun to kiss the nape of her neck.

And in seconds, somehow every ounce of anger and annoyance had slipped from her mind.

She still wasn't used to this. The feeling that she'd just swallowed a ten-pound bag of Pop Rocks or turned into one five-foot, ten-inch-tall circuit board. Her body transformed into a map of electrical nerve centers that fired off whenever Sam's mouth grazed hers, whenever his fingers touched her skin. Her reaction was so completely predictable: Sam came near, she went haywire. Every time. But its predictability didn't make it any less thrilling.

Before she knew it, they were collapsing onto Sam's bed, and Sam's arms were wrapping around her upper body. She kissed his neck, feeling the pulse beat against her lips.

"You are so beautiful," Sam murmured. His hand slid gently from her shoulders, caressing the exposed small of her back just below her T-shirt. Gaia's heart hammered. And as he brought his mouth to hers for a slow, deep kiss, she trembled. Nothing could be more perfect than this moment. Sam's kiss grew urgent, his palm tightening around Gaia's right hand, pressing it flat and smooth against the sheets on his bed.

"I want you," he whispered, his voice husky and full of need.

As if watching herself from afar, Gaia broke from the kiss. Her breath came fast. She gazed into Sam's beautifully kaleidoscopic, cut-glass eyes—the amber color burning with feeling and raw energy. Whatever had been worrying Sam seemed to have vanished. Now he was all passionate intensity and focus.

"I want you, too," she murmured in response. She wanted to be clear: *This* was the moment she'd been waiting for since she'd first laid eyes on Sam. The dingy room seemed to spin around her. *This is it,* she realized. A sweat broke on her palms. The time had come. Now. Apparently Gaia's life could have a good surprise, too, every now and then—not just an endless onslaught of betrayal and pain and violence spilling out of every gutter in the city.

Sam stared back at her, attentive.

"I'm ready," Gaia whispered. She brought a hand to Sam's strong jaw, traced the shape of it with her fingers. *This is it,* she said to herself once more. It seemed that all her life had been a climb to this peak of experience. It was the right time to lose her virginity to the one guy she knew she'd never regret loving.

Of course, she was also kind of skittery.

Not scared, obviously, since. . . well, yeah. . . but it was whatever came in a close second to fear: some nerve-splaying, bone-charging kind of anticipation that felt crazy and sane all at the same time.

Her eyes swept to the desk drawer. She knew Sam kept the condoms in there. They'd bought them together. Her face reddened a little—with a mixture of shyness and embarrassment but a desire to at least have them ready. *To be on the safe side. . .*

"No," Sam said. His voice seemed to float from nowhere.

Gaia turned to him, eyes wide. "What do you mean?" she asked. The words were little more than a whisper.

Sam smiled, catching her hand and bringing it to his lips. "That didn't sound right," he murmured.

"Gaia, you have to understand—of course I want to do this. It's all I ever think about, if you want to know the truth. But I also want the moment to be special. Not here in this hellhole room that I haven't cleaned for a week."

Gaia couldn't quite fathom the words. What was he so worried about? She'd been in this dump over a dozen times. She didn't need candles. Or flowers. She had no desire to know Victoria's Secret, and she had no need of any other tacky ceremonial shit. The act would speak for itself. All they needed was each other.

"The right moment?" Gaia asked, her voice breaking slightly. "Don't you know anything about me, Sam Moon? My life isn't exactly made up of right moments. I kind of have to take them where I can get them. . . ." She trailed off, threaded a hand through Sam's hair. Enough of this dillydallying already. She leaned closer to him.

Silently Sam covered Gaia's mouth with his, his teeth grazing her lower lip, his hand clamped firmly to the space between Gaia's shoulder blades. He didn't need to say anything. Gaia knew that he got it. Got her.

His weight pressed down on top of her, and for once Gaia felt small and delicate—not some hulking giant of a girl. She could feel the desire hammering there in his chest with every heartbeat. She found herself pulling Sam's shirt off over his head as he kissed her neck. She didn't think she could take much more of this. She was as ready as she would ever be, and every hope and prayer and even doubt and missed opportunity had converged and conspired to bring her to this moment—

Brring!

Crap.

Sam jerked up, narrowing his eyes.

"Ignore it," Gaia whispered, reaching for him.

But he didn't. With an apology flickering across his face, he jumped up off the bed and snatched up the phone—as if this were just any old moment that had just passed. As if they weren't about to make love for the first time. As if whoever was on the other end of the phone could really be so important. . . more important than the most beautiful moment in Gaia Moore's life to date. She couldn't believe it—

"Okay," Sam mumbled curtly into the receiver. He hung up without another word, then looked up at Gaia reluctantly. She could see sheepishness in his face and something else, too. Guilt. Well, good. He deserved to feel guilty. She swallowed, not quite sure how *she* was feeling. The excitement and urgency had faded, leaving only. . . emptiness. And a little anger as well.

"Who was it?" Gaia asked as nonchalantly as possible.

She sat up straight and smoothed down the bird's nest of hair.

He lowered his eyes. "Um, Keon," he said. "I have to go to the library. I. . . forgot we had a study date. God, I'm really sorry." His voice was low, and his expression had changed; it was still partly guilty, but there was now another emotion that Gaia couldn't place. For want of a better word, he just looked. . . strange. Strained and spaced out at the same time.

Gaia opened her mouth to say something, then thought better of it. A chill spread across her back as she fumbled for her sweatshirt on the floor. She felt suddenly like an idiot, like some soap opera cliché, panting at her man to ignore the phone when clearly he had other plans. Some dumb blonde. She would gladly bet Sam a hundred bucks that it wasn't Keon who had called. Sam was a lousy liar. But for whatever reason, he'd needed an excuse not to go through with the ultimate act at this moment.

Maybe you were just saved, an inner voice said as Gaia pushed herself out of the bed in silent anger. *Saved from wasting your virginity.* And Gaia had to concede that her inner voice had a point. Maybe Sam was right about wanting to wait. Maybe she should wait, too.

Maybe sex, that ultimate act of trust and knowing, wasn't such a good idea if your boyfriend was hiding things from you.

"GET READY TO SING WITH ME,
Eddie. *Get ready!*"

A Signature Event

Brian was growling in Ed's face as per usual, the veins bulging out of his tree-trunk neck, his face turning all shades of red. Ed still hadn't worked up the courage to ask Brian if he'd ever been a professional wrestler. It didn't seem much of a stretch—given his massive frame, his long black hair, and his apparent need to growl every single word at top volume. Yes. Ed's physical therapist might very well be insane, but he was also an ingenious motivator. Ed felt totally pumped at the end of every session.

Ed grasped the parallel bars that took up most of the available floor space in his room. His wheelchair stayed outside the door in the hall. It was fitting somehow. The chair had no place in here. Not anymore. This was where Ed walked. And where Shred rocked. Brian threw a CD into the stereo and flipped the volume knob. The deafening crunch of some vaguely familiar rap-metal band burst from the speakers.

"Let's make some *noise,* Eddie!" Brian shouted.

For a second Ed almost felt like laughing—at least until the sweat broke on his forehead. As the music blared, Ed took one painstakingly slow, agonizing "step" at a time. They weren't really steps; he supported all his weight with his arms. The hope was that by standing upright, his newly improved legs would get used to the position. The pain was awful, shooting through his arms. But he welcomed it. Because the moment he felt that same pain in his legs, he knew he would be halfway recovered.

Brian spotted him but never supported him. Ed's red face began to drip as he moved farther and farther toward the end of the bars. Just a few more feet. . .

"Come on, Eddie!" Brian hollered. "One more step! Do it for Wes Borland, baby. That guy *rocks*."

Ed pushed himself to take another step. *Wes Borland?* He had no idea what Brian was talking about, of course—but then, he rarely did.

"You're doing it, you stud," Brian encouraged him, literally spitting in Ed's ear. "Now bring it on back. You're rock-and-roll *lightning,* baby!"

Ed's heart pounded in time with the music. He grinned through the agony as he began his journey back across the bars—moaning with every aching maneuver and loving every minute of it. He focused on the goals, the final results of all this torture: walking down the street without anyone staring at him for a change, getting on the bus via the *front* door, a dance with Heather, a walk with Gaia, anything else with Gaia. . . just standing next to Gaia. . . .

And then he felt something.

Something big. Something he definitely hadn't felt before.

There was a huge tingling sensation running down his *entire* left leg.

He shook the leg ever so slightly—which is to say, his brain told the leg to shake, and the leg *shook*.

"Holy shit!" Ed screamed.

"What's up, dude?" Brian yelled back with a massive grin. "Did you feel something? Tell me you freakin' felt something, *baby!*"

But Ed was too jubilant for words. The pain was forgotten. It was happening. It was actually happening! It wasn't a dream; it wasn't an illusion. He'd moved his legs! A wave of sheer ecstasy washed over him as he realized the truth—that the surgery *had* been a success, that his work *was* paying off, that he would and could *walk again*. . . that Brian was truly a genius.

"I. . .!"

And then Ed stopped himself. He stopped himself cold, before he let himself utter another word. At that moment all the ecstasy spilled out of his body—as swiftly as if a plug had been pulled. He was left with a numb void. A black hole in the center of his chest. Because he couldn't tell Brian what had just happened. He couldn't tell anyone. The only person he could tell probably didn't even want to hear it. And for one split second Ed truly hated Heather—for the lies, for the deception, for the promises she'd forced on him.

She'd just robbed him of one of the most amazing moments of his life.

"Eddie?" Brian growled over the music. "Did you feel something?"

In spite of everything inside him, against all his better judgment, Ed managed to shake his head. "No," he said almost inaudibly. "I thought I did. . . ."

"What?" Brian squawked. "Well, if you thought you did, you *did*."

"No," Ed insisted. The pain returned a hundredfold. His entire body weakened. His arms began to shake from holding up all his body weight. So Ed let himself collapse to the ground. He didn't know what else to do. He was barely conscious of tumbling to the floor. Brian flipped off the music and helped Ed back to his feet, helping him get a grip on the parallel bars.

"Well, let's keep moving, dude," Brian shouted. "We'll get there, bro—"

"No," Ed interrupted. "I'm tired, Brian. I think I've got to stop for today."

There was a long silence. Brian stared at him. Ed could feel Brian's disappointment; the guy wasn't one to conceal his emotions. It made Ed sick with humiliation. This was the first sign of negativity Ed had ever shown, and Brian knew it was nothing like him. Of

all the goddamn irony in the world. . .
the greatest thing yet had just
happened—and he felt worse than he'd
ever felt. All thanks to Heather.

"Okay," Brian said simply. He didn't scream. He almost sounded like a normal human being, which was somehow deeply upsetting. "Hey. We all get tired, Eddie. Maybe you'll feel better tomorrow."

"Maybe," Ed mumbled, unable to look him in the eye.

Brian grabbed his coat and headed for the door. He wasn't one for long good-byes, but this one was particularly short.

"Later," Brian said. His footsteps faded down the hall.

Ed gripped the parallel bars, shaking with frustration, staring at his wheelchair in the hall. His feelings for Heather usually ran so deep.

But not at this moment.

No, right now Ed was just seething with anger, and all he could think about was one thing: *Heather doesn't want me to walk. Heather would rather have my money than have me walk.* He clenched his fists together for fear he might hit something. Lash out and break a bone or a piece of furniture. He clenched his fists together—

And then suddenly Ed realized the significance of this action.

As he felt his nails digging into his palms, he realized his hands. . . *were at his sides.*

He was no longer gripping the bars. Yet he was still standing.

He looked down at his feet.

At that moment Ed Fargo hit the floor again.

It's funny how nothing ever stays the same. Nothing. For the longest time it seemed like I was untouchable. After everything I went through when Ed had his accident, after all that sorrow and guilt and heartache, I made a pact with myself: that I'd never sink to that level of sadness again. That no matter what, I'd always stay on top.

And I did. Even through all that stuff with Sam. Even when Gaia Moore blew into my life and my relationship with Sam fell apart, I still kept it together on the outside. Think of a swan gliding across a pond. There's all that furious web-footed churning under the surface, but all you see is the bird gliding by, unruffled. On top of it all. On the surface, at least.

That was me.

On top of things, placidly gliding across the surface without messing up a feather. Up where I belonged. Or at least where everyone else seemed to think I belonged.

But now I feel like I'm cracking. Ed's keeping me at arm's length; Phoebe isn't getting any better; my parents are penniless. And I'm finding it hard to stay afloat. Watching my parents and Phoebe, I'm beginning to think that life has no patterns. It's just a series of arbitrary circumstances, some good, some bad. All of it meaningless and random.

I've also decided that what doesn't kill you doesn't necessarily make you stronger, either. Every knock adds up. Sooner or later, you sink.

Worst of all, I can't talk to anyone about this stuff. It's not like my friends would even begin to understand or empathize. And I can't talk to my parents. They're in even worse shape.

Once upon a time Ed was that person, the one person I could tell anything to, no matter how harsh. But he's too busy shutting me out to care. And besides, he's too full of optimism right now to even begin to relate—too filled with his recovery to see how my life is breaking up into chunks and sinking.

I am totally alone. It's like that book *The Stranger*. Maybe Camus is right. Maybe life is just an existential exercise. I still don't think I quite get what existential means, but it sounds lonely and hideous, and that's exactly how life is.

For the first time ever, I feel I'm getting dangerously close to numb.

Here's another thing that makes no sense: How can a person feel so desperately unhappy, yet-feel numb at the exact same time? Numbness is like the opposite of sadness. Or is it? Nothing makes sense.

The only thing I know is that I don't give a shit anymore about the things that used to matter to me. It's hard work even getting

dressed in the morning, never
mind color coordinating.

   I don't even care that Gaia
and Sam are rumored to be a
couple.

   I have bigger things to worry
about than that.

Even *with* a knife, these two were about as intimidating **black letters** as a couple of stuffed animals.

"DAD, THIS PLACE IS A JOKE,"

Blending In

Gaia complained, her eyes darting from side to side as she stood at the entrance of Antique Boutique, the primo FOH shopping stop. She just knew she would run into Megan or Tina or Heather herself. And the last people Gaia felt like seeing were the Kate-Spade-toting, Tommy-reeking, self-designated in crowd who had placed themselves at the top of the Village School's limited social pyramid.

It was kind of funny: For the first time since they'd reunited, Gaia actually found she was annoyed with her father. But she supposed that was a good sign. Teenage daughters were supposed to get annoyed with their dads, right?

"Gaia, you swore you'd let me take you on a shopping spree and buy you some new clothes," he mumbled. "Besides, what's wrong with this place?" He lowered his dark glasses and gave the boutique a piercing, blue-eyed once-over. "It looks. . . fashionable." The word seemed to catch in his throat.

Before Gaia could point out that he was clearly as miserable as she was, an overly excited salesman shot up like a jack-in-the-box from under a counter in the bag check.

"Can I check your coat?" he demanded. Then he turned away and whined something incomprehensible into the headset squeezed tightly to his Roman-page-boy hairdo.

"It's like a military operation in here," Tom joked.

Gaia rolled her eyes and yanked her father back onto Broadway, into cold air and the late afternoon fading light.

"Listen, I think I understand why you don't want to do this," Tom said in a gently chiding voice. "You don't feel like conforming. That's what I love about you; you never feel a need to be anyone but yourself. But there's a difference between conforming and blending in."

"There is?" she muttered. But her tone was only half serious. If her father wanted to play Dad, she figured she might as well indulge him. After all, they were still making up for five years of lost time—years that could never be restored, no matter how hard they tried.

She allowed him to lead her into the store next door, which was, admittedly, better. It was still trendy, but there were no squeaking salesmen, no obvious brand names worthy of FOH attention. Just shelves full of sweaters and a couple of dresses. *Blending in.* Gaia repeated the words to herself and snorted as she pictured herself trying to become a part of the scene that the likes of Heather operated in: a bubble of cuteness and best-friends-forever shit.

"You know, I don't have to remind you that blending

in is how I've managed to stay alive," her father remarked mildly, as if sensing Gaia's thought processes. "I'm not suggesting you take an alias or wear a fake mustache. I'm just suggesting you buy a nice skirt. Give those two ragged sweatshirts of yours a rest. Here, why don't you try on this dress?"

Gaia shot her father an amused smirk as his eyes flashed from the pale green dress on the wall to her gray hooded sweatshirt. He shrugged, as if to say: *See?*

"Trust me, Dad, I would *not* blend in if I showed up at school in this dress." She adopted a mock-serious tone. "I'd upset the delicate balance of the fragile adolescent society in which I live."

Her father laughed.

"Not to mention the fact that I'd look like a two-ton heifer trying to squeeze into an ice-skater's outfit," she added quietly.

"Gaia, please," he argued, smiling. "You're seventeen. You're beautiful. Try on the dress. You wouldn't be upsetting any delicate balance. Lots of kids your age wear that dress, I'm sure. And you know the old cliché: *Quando a Roma. . .*"

Gaia groaned as she pushed aside the curtain of a changing-room cubicle. *When in Rome. . .* Funny. If only her father had the slightest clue what he was talking about. Now that she thought about it, this normal stuff had the potential to get on her nerves—what with shopping with Dad and lectures on self-esteem. Scowling, she lost her sweatshirt and pants, then shimmied into the green dress.

When she looked at herself in the mirror, she thanked God that she was born with no fear gene. Otherwise her reflection would have terrified her. For starters, the dress was way too short for her way-too-long legs. It was also too tight across what she saw as her overdeveloped shoulders and muscle-bound stomach. No doubt about it: Even in this ridiculous getup, she was still several Grand Canyon–sized leaps away from feminine. Forget about looking like an ice-skater. She had a better shot at being mistaken for a female boxer.

Oh, well. Sighing, Gaia took one last, punishing look at herself and wondered why she'd even bothered *attempting* to be a regular girl. This dress was made for a baby-doll teen, the kind of girl who screamed for boy bands. Couldn't her father see that—

"Are you sure this shit isn't alarmed?" a voice whispered in the cubicle next to hers.

Gaia stiffened at the sound. Then suddenly she felt very depressed. That was just another one of her abnormal qualities—an animal-like sense of hearing.

"Who cares? Let's get out of here," a second voice retorted.

Without a moment's hesitation Gaia stepped out of her cubicle—just in time to see two girls pull back the curtain of their own. One was small and sallow with bad skin and a frightened, guilty look on her face. Her backpack was bursting at the seams. It probably weighed as much as she did. The other was a big, broad goth-metal girl—more beef than fat, with a pierced lip, a pierced eyebrow, and sullen eyes.

Gaia planted herself in front of them.

The goth chick flashed her a don't-mess-with-me look.

"I don't think you want to leave without hanging up the stuff you just tried on," Gaia said pleasantly, her eyes falling on the bulging backpack of the smaller girl.

"And I don't think you want to butt into anyone's business," the bigger girl shot back, her mouth twisting into an ugly half smile, half grimace.

"Oh, but you're wrong." Gaia blocked the exit with a long arm as she leaned against the wall. "Butting in is what I like to do."

"Well, then how come your butt is hanging *out* of that heinous dress?" the small girl demanded. And then, to Gaia's utter shock, she reached into her bag and pulled out a switchblade—which she promptly flicked open and wielded in Gaia's face. "Now get the hell out of my way, bitch."

Normally Gaia would have laughed. Even *with* a knife, these two were about as intimidating as a couple of stuffed animals. But she was extremely pissed. She wasn't sure which was more infuriating, being called a bitch by the sidekick of a Marilyn Manson wanna-be or the comment about the dress. No, actually, she *was* sure. The dress. Definitely the comment about the dress. Gaia cursed herself for having even tried it on. She had to get out of it. Now. But first, of course, she'd have to deal with these very unfortunate half-wits.

The smaller girl lunged forward, blade out. Gaia simply stepped out of her way; she didn't even have to make much effort to dodge the strike. The girl had telegraphed it before she'd even moved. With her left hand Gaia feinted a punch. With her right she jabbed a quick punch into the girl's midsection. The girl gasped, doubling over. The goth's jaw dropped as the knife slipped from the smaller one's fingers. Gaia calmly picked up the knife and raised her eyebrows.

"Now, I know you don't want me to break every bone in your body," she stated. "That'll make shoplifting so much more difficult."

The smaller girl collapsed onto the floor, clutching her stomach. The goth girl took a step back. Gaia smiled. Suddenly an anxious store clerk appeared, followed by her father and a security guard. Her father surveyed the scene, then grinned. Gaia shrugged. She noticed a security camera above his head. The store employees must have seen the whole fight. Gaia glanced back at the girls. They must have seen the camera, too. And they had still attacked her with a knife. Geniuses, they were not.

"Are you all right?" her father asked. He sounded almost amused. He knew a shoplifter with a switchblade was no great threat to his daughter—which, of course, was just another perfect example of how she could never possibly "blend in."

"See what happens when I put on a dress?" she asked.

Tom chuckled. "Well, I think you look beautiful."

"Sure, you do." She patted his shoulder, feeling mildly sick. "I'll go get my sweatshirt."

PLEASE, GAIA, DON'T MAKE ONE OF *your territorial walks around Washington Square,* Sam prayed as he stood under a scraggly tree in the park. *Not now.*

Sam felt a chill underneath his coat. He looked around warily, gripping the package that Josh had ordered him to pick up from outside a garment factory in Hell's Kitchen. So this was what it had come down to: Josh gives Sam one alibi; Josh gets a permanent messenger boy in return. This was the third "errand" Sam had agreed to run for Josh. He'd just about had it. He could feel his sanity slipping away—not only because of the humiliation, but because of the damage it was doing to his relationship with Gaia.

The cold air stung his face. He knew that a relationship with the opposite sex was all about building trust. He knew it all too well. After all, lack of trust was one of the contributing factors that had destroyed his relationship with Heather. And here he was telling Gaia these stupid white lies so he could run his errands, praying he wouldn't run into her? It was infuriating. Not to mention pathetic.

There was no way he was going to do another one of these deliveries. He'd more than paid Josh back already. He'd simply made the wrong friend in a very messed up set of circumstances, and now he'd paid the price. Hopefully this would be the last of the deliveries—and then they'd be even, no questions asked, and Sam could say good-bye to Josh permanently.

Hopefully.

Sam glanced around the park. Nobody was showing to pick up the package. In fact, he barely saw anyone at all. Just a few bits of garbage blowing in circles, as if stirring up a fuss to demand that somebody clean them up. He couldn't remember the last time the park had been this still at 6:00 P.M. The chess tables stood vacant. The benches glistened and dripped with melting ice. The fountain was silent and ghostly, lit up by a wrought-iron lamp nearby. Silhouettes of trees looked like scarecrows in the dimness of early evening.

He swallowed.

Where was his contact? Out of his peripheral vision he spotted movement. But it was only a group of young girls, straggling across one of the paths. The clatter of their boots echoed and died, and again the park was deathly silent. Sam jiggled from one foot to the other. A palpable fear was coagulating in his veins.

And then suddenly he materialized.

A dark shape appeared in the shadows, walking straight toward Sam.

Make that a she.

Sam's eyes widened. The massive, hulking figure was a woman. . . technically speaking. The curves were all in place and undeniable, but this person could easily crush Sam into the ground with one overhand punch. Some battle of chromosomes had been lost— or the outcome purposefully fixed. He couldn't help but shrink away a little as she stopped in front of him. Her face was concealed by a scarf.

"Got something for me?" she whispered, her hands jammed into the pockets of a black ski jacket. Her voice was deep, raspy.

Sam's heart pounded. Where did Josh find these people? Not that it mattered. There was no point in prolonging this encounter any longer than necessary. Getting out of the park as fast as was humanly possible seemed the smartest option. He handed over the package and turned to go.

"Slow down, *homey.*" The woman stopped Sam with a rough hand on his shoulder, then pulled him back and thrust an eight-by-eleven manila envelope into his hands. "It's a drop-off *and* a pickup."

Sam stumbled backward. His fear mounted. He didn't know exactly what kind of trouble this was, but he could smell that something was off. He should go. Now. But then she took a sudden step toward him— and he dropped the package, his fists clenched at his sides, ready to defend himself. The park was still as empty and eerie as it had been when he arrived. If something happened to him, no one would see it. A metallic taste of fear coated the roof of his mouth. The woman's eyes were only inches from Sam's face now—as lifeless as the park itself. Instantly Sam's mind was on alert. He sorted options for defense and attack.

But then she laughed and stepped back. "Just wanted to read what was on your hat," she said. Reflexively Sam's hand went to the NYU knitted cap pulled low over his forehead. "Keep your grades up," she whispered, then turned and disappeared into the park without another word.

Relief exploded from Sam's rib cage in a shaky

series of gasps. He took a moment to collect himself, shaking his head and staring into the darkness. He swore under his breath several times. He couldn't take this anymore.

Finally, when his pulse and breathing had reached seminormal states, he bent down and picked up the envelope.

SAM MOON

Sam blinked. That couldn't be right. . . but the words were there. In black letters. He'd been expecting the address of some warehouse or Josh's name on the package. But this package was personally addressed to Sam. He ripped the tab on the envelope. Bits of colored paper fell to his feet, rustled by a gust of wind. Photographs. Sam knelt and picked them up, and as his eyes fell on one of them, his face froze.

Gaia.

Or rather Gaia and *him.*

In his bed.

Her blond hair fanned out across his chest. His arms were wrapped around her naked back. A black cloud descended over Sam's thoughts as he thumbed through the other pictures. They were all variations on the same intimate theme, spelled out in a string of Kodak moments. His fingers began to shake—so violently that he couldn't handle the pictures anymore. He sat down on a bench and tried to think. To deal. To stomach the obvious color-printed truth in his hands. Someone had been spying on him and Gaia. Someone had actually photographed them.

He shoved a hand into the envelope to see if there was more. Just a slip of paper with a neatly typed message in all caps: HANDS OFF.

Sam dropped the note to the ground. Memories of that early morning phone call flashed through his head once more.

Don't touch her, or you'll be sorry.

The note blew away in the wind. That was it. He shot up from the bench and turned in circles, again and again, searching the park for any sign of his enemy. Or was it enemies? The possibilities were too overwhelming. Were they watching him right now? And who were *they*? One thing was for sure: *They* were not some prank caller. *They* were for real. He dropped back down to the bench and tried to steady himself. *Stay calm,* he shouted inside his own head, his heart beating a mile a minute, his mouth as dry as the wind.

How did they know I'd be here? No, what am I saying? They didn't just know I'd be here; they sent me here just to get their message. Josh sent me here—

A series of questions flashed through Sam's mind. What was Josh doing in his room that morning? How long had he been there? Where did he go right before Sam got the phone call? All of Sam's fears of the last few weeks—every one of his "bad feelings," every one of the vague doubts and unsettling premonitions. . . they were all falling together to form one huge and terrifying conclusion. A conclusion that Sam had really known all along.

Whoever *they* were, Josh was one of them.

And Josh was in control.

To: J
From: L
Date: February 12
File: 776244
Subject: Gaia Moore
Last seen: Broadway, 3:44 p.m.

Continue to monitor subject at close range.
Keep subject away from the Messenger.
Request status report re essentials required
for party.

To: L
From: J
Date: February 12
File: 776244
Subject: Gaia Moore
Last seen: Broadway, 3:44 p.m.

Subject and Messenger are being closely moni-
tored. All party plans are moving swiftly. Expect
further communications via the Messenger.

Maybe it's possible that men have a "time of the month" just like women. I once heard a theory that males have testosterone surges that affect their moods, but I always thought it was a bunch of crap. Now I'm not so sure. It might explain the weird-ness of the two most important guys in my life (aside from my father, of course): Sam and Ed.

Okay, maybe not Ed's. My first guess is that things aren't so hot between Ed and Heather. He's been pretty icy to her of late. So maybe Heather is why he's totally humorless these days. But he won't tell me anything, so I don't know for sure. All I know is that he's acting very peculiar—jittery and distant and generally un-Fargo in all ways.

As for Sam, I have no theories there. Except for the lame-assed hormonal one. But I do know beyond the shadow of a doubt that something is up with him. I know what it's like to be on the

receiving end of caginess. It's
not like I'm unfamiliar with
secrecy in a relationship, of
course. But only my own.

Yes, that's hypocritical. But
it's also the truth. And I never
lie. Which is another reason this
whole trend disturbs me. Both Sam
and Ed are lying to me. About
what, I don't know. But maybe
this is my punishment. Maybe this
is karma: the whole what-goes-
around-comes-around part of existence. For once I'm happy and my
life is out in the open—but now
everyone else is acting weird and
keeping secrets.

Or maybe this is just what
life looks like from a happy person's perspective.

If so, happiness is overrated.

This one had
close-cropped
bangs and was
more
overweight **pretty**
than muscular.
She also had **boy**
a lazy, milky
eye that
drifted to
the side.

SAM HAD NO IDEA HOW LONG

Checkmate

he'd been standing outside Josh's closed door. Minutes, definitely... possibly longer. But he was frozen solid, still as a statue in the sickly yellow light of their suite. There was nothing to be done. As a chess player, Sam knew the certainty of defeat very well: that one clear moment when your opponent had cut off all options. And even if Josh was in there, what could Sam possibly say, given the circumstances? He was utterly powerless. One wrong move and he was in jail for life. Checkmate.

So he stood by the door with his heart in his throat and his chest constricted until Josh opened it himself.

"Sammy!" Josh greeted Sam with a slap on the shoulder and his usual grin. Sam couldn't believe he'd once found that perfect smile reassuring. Now it made him sick. "I thought I heard somebody out there. Come on in. How was the delivery?"

For a split second Sam thought about punching him in the face, knocking him cold, strangling him. But he couldn't move. He couldn't even look at the guy—dressed in the old sweat suit he always wore, as if he truly were just another ordinary RA at NYU. Sam couldn't bring himself to look anywhere but his shoes.

"Did you get your package?" Josh asked.

Sam's head jerked up. He shot daggers at Josh with his eyes. He couldn't believe it. He was dealing with a true sociopath. Which meant that Josh was more dangerous than Sam had imagined. Which only made Sam more frightened.

"Did you?" Josh pressed, his voice hardening.

Again Sam remained silent.

"I'm sure you did." Josh opened his closet door and pulled a box from it with an envelope attached. "Now, this one's not going to be too pleasant." He handed the box to Sam. "I need you to take this to the Manhattan federal jail. Just go through the visitors' entrance. Your contact will find you right inside the door. The details are in the envelope, okay? Are we cool?"

Cool? Come on! Say something! Find another move! There's got to be another move—

"Hello?" Josh laughed. It sounded like the bark of a cruel dog. "Earth to Sammy. Are we cool?"

"Yes," Sam replied, his heart flooding with futility. It was the first time he'd spoken in hours. The word was dry, hoarse.

"Excellent. See you soon." Josh sat at his desk and opened a notebook, as if Sam were being dismissed.

Sam turned around and walked halfway through

the doorway. But something stopped him. He wasn't sure what it was—rage, maybe. Either that or panic. But he whirled and turned back to Josh.

"Josh?"

"Yeah, what's up?"

"I need to know. . . ." Sam wasn't even sure what he wanted to say. Maybe he was just praying that there was some stitch of common decency somewhere inside this coldhearted bastard. "Who's doing this? It can't be just you. Who are you working for? Who hates me so much?"

Josh shook his head, his eyes buried in the notebook. "You don't need to know that," he mumbled.

"I just. . . I just want to know why."

"Don't get philosophical on me," Josh warned in an annoying, jokey tone.

"No, please." Sam clenched his jaw. "Why? Why me?"

Suddenly the smile dropped completely from Josh's face. He snapped the notebook shut and stared coldly into Sam's eyes.

"Ours is not to reason why, Sam. Do I need to finish that proverb for you?"

Sam felt ice in his veins. "No," he said. He turned away and left the room with a sense of horror that was totally new to him—a kind of dread he'd never experienced. No, Josh didn't need to finish the sentence. Sam's dad used to quote it all the time.

Ours is not to reason why. . . ours is but to do and die.

"BRIEF ME." GAIA HELD UP A COPY

No Reason

of Albert Camus's *The Stranger* as Ed slammed his locker shut. "I haven't read it."

That wasn't entirely true. Gaia had actually read the classic in its original French with her father when she was twelve years old, but she couldn't remember it as well as her teacher would want. Her mother had been killed shortly thereafter. The first line was what she recalled most vividly: *Maman est morte.* Mother is dead.

It hit a little too close to home.

As they walked to MacGregor's class, Gaia stared at the cover of the thin book: a desert scene with a silhouetted figure of a man in the distance. It was a short novel. She could easily have reread it the night before. *If* she hadn't wasted so much mental energy trying to figure out Sam's problem. Or Ed's. But at least in Ed's case, she'd come to some conclusion: Patience was the best bet. A great virtue. *But not one of mine.* Still, Ed being Ed, he was bound to spill sooner or later.

"It's about a man who kills another man for no reason," Ed said as he wheeled himself down the hallway.

"That much I knew." Gaia stole a sideways look at Ed, hunched over in his wheelchair as he maneuvered his way through the traffic of floating Jansport bags and Diesel jeans. His eyes gave nothing away, but his tight jaw betrayed the tension lurking beneath. Gaia knew that was about all she'd get from Ed in silent mode. He'd barely even looked at her, much less volunteered any clues as to what was happening with him.

"It's about the absurdity, expendability, and randomness of life," Ed continued in an oddly intense tone, still staring ahead.

"Camus should have been a movie director," Gaia joked.

But Ed didn't reply, didn't even register that she'd spoken. His eyes were on something else. Someone else. Gaia felt a sinking feeling in her stomach, sensing who it was even before she saw that unmistakable brown hair and teen supermodel face.

"Hi, Ed."

Heather paused as Ed slowed to greet her. She didn't even acknowledge Gaia's existence. Which was fine with Gaia. She hung back a little. She was not in the mood for a witchy Gannis greeting, not so early in the day. Nor did she feel like witnessing a broad Heather-to-Ed beaming smile.

"Hi," Ed answered. His voice was flat.

For once Heather seemed less than composed. Her hair was kind of tousled, now that Gaia took a good look at it. And her eyes were puffy.

"Did you finish the book?" Heather asked Ed.

"Yes."

"I nearly finished it."

"Oh. Well, you should. It's worth reading."

Gaia knit her brow. *What the hell?* They were talking like a couple of androids, lobbing impersonal quasi-pleasantries back and forth. Only a slight tremor at Heather's lower lip betrayed any feeling at all. For his part, Ed was totally without emotion, unless you could call stilted awkwardness an emotion.

Ed glanced up at Gaia. "We should get to class."

"Uh. . . yeah." Gaia nodded, waiting for Heather to strike. Whenever Ed addressed Gaia directly in Heather's presence, it inevitably elicited some scathing insult. But there was nothing. And Gaia knew she looked like crap this morning, having slept badly and woken up late. Circles under the eyes. A threadbare pair of puke-green cords and a sweatshirt that was bravely attempting to hold itself together at the seams. Hair a mess. Overall, she knew she looked like she'd been dragged backward through a bush. An easy target for Heather.

But in a Village School first, Heather didn't say a word.

And for the first time in her life Gaia *wished* Heather would insult her, thus reassuring Gaia that all was well with the universe and the logical order of things hadn't been completely tossed out the window.

Instead Heather just sighed.

The three of them silently filed into MacGregor's classroom. Ed immediately made for a space at the back, surrounded on all sides. No room for Heather. Or Gaia. Like an automaton, Heather sat down next to the FOHs. Gaia slouched into the first vacant spot she could see, still trying to process the schizoid scenario she'd just witnessed. She knew she wouldn't get an answer from Ed. No, Ed had closed himself off to the world—as tightly as Gaia herself had in the very first weeks she had arrived in New York.

"And here we have our protagonist, Meursault...," MacGregor opened.

Gaia stared at the blackboard, her muddled, irritable thoughts punctuated in short intervals by MacGregor's words. Words like *disconnected* and *alienated*.

More than ever, Gaia felt she could relate.

I SHOULD JUST GET OUT OF HERE.

But it wasn't an option. Sam's feet carried him through the forbidding metal doors of the visitors' entrance of the Manhattan federal jail—a dank spot in the bowels of lower

Penance

Manhattan, virtually hidden from the sidewalk by a long, descending staircase. As soon as the doors slammed behind him, he froze. A metal detector blocked further entry into the facility. His grip tightened around the package. His skin was clammy with sweat, but he couldn't tell if he was hot or cold. Anxiety had scraped his nerves raw. He had no idea where he was going or who he was supposed to meet. The instructions hadn't said a thing about his contact. Sam could only picture trying to walk through the metal detector and setting it off—then being apprehended for whatever horrible stuff was concealed in this box—

A woman in a prison guard uniform suddenly appeared from behind the security station and strode toward him. Sam sucked in an extra hit of oxygen. *Her.* That woman from the park. His pulse slammed into overdrive—but then his eyes narrowed. Or. . . not. This one had close-cropped bangs and was more overweight than muscular. She also had a lazy, milky eye that drifted to the side. Sam shuddered. What kind of a place was this?

She stopped right in front of him. He looked at her. A curt nod was the only signal she gave. But that was all he needed. He handed over the package.

"Better get out of here," she said, weighing the package in her hands, her good eye boring into Sam. "This is no place for a pretty boy like you."

Sam blinked. His stomach squeezed. Without pausing for another breath, he turned and bolted out the doors—nearly tripping on the stairwell, using his hands to propel him up the last few steps. There were no words to describe his revulsion: at that guard, at himself, at the stale jail air. *No place for a pretty boy.* The words conjured up images too sordid to ponder.

He kept running as he hit the street, sprinting toward the nearest subway station. His heart knocked at his rib cage. He blinked rapidly, feeling the weight of tears behind his eyes.

Why is this happening? Why was everything falling apart, just when it had started to come together? But just as fast as self-pity swooped in, Sam felt the familiar gnaw of guilt. He was ashamed to feel so sorry for himself. At least he could feel *something.* Mike Suarez didn't have that option anymore. Maybe this whole situation—the mess with the police, the bribes, the photographs, the mysterious enemy— was his penance for Mike. Maybe that voice on the phone hadn't been lying. Maybe that voice really *was* a messenger from beyond the grave.

In which case, Sam might have to heed the voice's warnings—even the ones that told him to keep away from Gaia.

To: J
From: L
Date: February 13
File: 001
Subject: Dinner party

Plans for the party progressing. Invitations have gone out. Costumes have been delivered. More to follow.

Why I believe I will walk again:
- The doctors are optimistic.
- I stood up.

Why I believe I won't walk again:
- Doctors are optimistic by trade.
- I fell down.

Ashen faced,
he opened
his mouth,
apparently
freaking
searching
for the **posers**
right words
to say. As if
there could
be any.

GAIA NODDED COOLLY FROM THE
fountain as Sam waved from
the miniature Arc de Triomphe.
He ran toward her, smiling.

The Boyfriend-Girlfriend Thing

"Hey," she called. But her
voice betrayed her lack of
enthusiasm. Her eyes were on
the dry fountain bed, where
old brown pennies lay like bits
of dirt—dead wishes from
some long-ago summer, when
the water had incited people
to throw their change away so
that their dreams could come
true. *As if it could make a difference.*

And then Sam was right in front of her. Gaia stiffened her neck and moved almost imperceptibly so
that Sam's mouth found her cheek and not her lips.
He had suggested a walk after school instead of their
usual get-together at his dorm. And as usual, he didn't
give any reason for the change in plans.

More secrets. More deception.

"How's it going?" he asked.

"Fine," she lied.

She hated lying. Until very recently she'd
made a hard-and-fast rule for herself: Always tell the
truth, or don't say anything at all. But that had been
back when she was alone, on her own, with no

attachments. She realized she'd learned a lesson. The closer you got to people, the more you had to lie. It was sick.

Sam stared at her. He opened his mouth as if to say something, then sighed. Gaia shook her head. Maybe he didn't want to lie anymore, either, so he was just shutting up as well. She stuffed her hands inside her fleece jacket. She and Sam remained silent as they headed out of the park and south, over to Bleecker Street. Gaia concentrated on the drab gray concrete beneath her feet. It was so confusing: Until now they'd grabbed every available moment of privacy so they could explore the intimate side of their relationship— keeping the world out because nothing mattered except their being together. Until now.

He doesn't want to be alone with me.

Or maybe there was another reason. Gaia desperately wanted to believe there was some palatable explanation for why Sam would rather walk the streets than be alone with Gaia behind closed doors—some reason that didn't produce a mental gag reflex. But all she could come up with were pitiful joke theories. Like maybe Sam needed fresh air after all that "studying" and "lab work" and "oversleeping." *Sure.*

"Let's go into Chinatown," Sam suggested as they banked east toward Lafayette. "I haven't been there in a long time."

Gaia searched Sam's face. His eyes were glassy as marbles, unchanging. Vacant. His skin was so pale, it was almost translucent, the few freckles on his nose standing out as if they'd been made with a Sharpie. He kept looking over his shoulder, too. Why? Was he doing something wrong by walking the streets with his girlfriend?

"What's the matter with you?" Gaia found herself asking. She stopped in her tracks. Her tolerance meter had reached its capacity. The time had come to end this lame charade before they spent an afternoon walking in empty circles, going nowhere.

"Nothing. It's. . . I'm sorry," Sam murmured. "Please, Gaia, let's just walk, okay?"

"You know what?" Gaia heard herself ask, as if she were listening to somebody else. "I don't really want to hang out right now."

Sam searched her face. "What?"

"I think I'd just rather walk by myself," she said, walking faster.

"But we. . ." Sam didn't finish.

She lengthened her stride and pushed down Lafayette, banging past a huddle of German tourists, weaving through a band of Pokémon-backpacked children—leaving Sam behind. For a fleeting instant she honestly didn't care if he caught up.

"Hey!" Sam shouted feebly behind her.

"I'll see you later!" she called, and her voice caught. She couldn't handle the pain anymore. She broke into a jog, whipping past delis and shoe stores. Street signs blurred as misery rose up inside her. It felt good to run, to have adrenaline flowing through her, to feel icy air tear into her lungs. She would run and run and run—

"Stop!" Sam shouted.

He was right behind her now. She tried to speed up, but he careened past her on Spring Street, throwing himself in front of her to break her stride. She knew she could sidestep him and keep going. She had plenty of physical steam left in her. But there seemed no point to that, either. Because she'd outrun even her own motivation for running. Where was she going? Nowhere. That was the whole point. She could get away from Sam, but she couldn't outrun her problems.

"Gaia. Please listen." Sam panted as he ran a hand through his hair. "I. . . need you to wait."

"For what?" Gaia groaned.

"For. . . me." The words came in a tired sigh.

Gaia folded her arms across her chest. What did he think she'd been doing this whole time? For weeks? For *months*. Once again she couldn't bring herself to look at him. She stared stone-faced past his head, over to a strip of sidewalk vendors attempting to push their phony Rolex watches and Prada bags onto a flock of bland-looking tourists. Any idiot would know that the merchandise was fake. It was no secret. But people bought the stuff, anyway, because they were a bunch of freaking posers. Everybody was. Suddenly the whole world seemed pointless, just a place for pretense.

"Give it up," Gaia mumbled. Her throat constricted. Her rage melted away, overcome with an aching sadness. "Stop pretending you care when you don't. Stop pretending to be someone you're not. If you don't want to go out with me, then say so. I can take it. I've dealt with a lot worse stuff in my life."

Sam winced. "Is that what you think?" He gasped, shaking his head. "That I don't want to go out with you? How can—"

"What am I supposed to think?" Gaia shoved a fistful of hair away from her face, but the wind whipped it right back in front of her. "You hide things from me. You make things up. And now you're trying to avoid having me in your dorm. . ." She couldn't finish. Her voice was too strained. And there was no way she would allow herself to cry.

"You've got it all wrong," Sam whispered.

Gaia laughed miserably. "Then are you going to tell me what's going on? Because I can't do this anymore. I can't. . . pretend."

Sam nodded. He looked weak and unsteady. "I know. But I can't tell you. I can only tell you that I need some space here." He opened his mouth to add more, then apparently thought better of it.

"But why?" Gaia choked out. She didn't deserve this. And there was no way she could explain this freakish behavior away with sympathy. Whatever was turning Sam into a shell of his former self was bigger than his grief over Mike. She knew that now.

"Look," Sam replied, taking a step toward her. "Please trust me, Gaia. This has nothing to do with us. I'm going through some personal stuff. Something I need to sort out by myself."

"Fine. Then go through it. Just leave me out if it until you're done, okay?"

Gaia turned and walked. Sadness gave way to anger once more. *She* had opened up to him about her life, her father and their tentative new dress rehearsal for a normal life, her uncle— everything. But apparently he couldn't reciprocate. Maybe she'd even scared him off by opening up too much. Now, *that* was funny. A grim smile spread across her face as she strode down Broadway, turning east along Canal, heading for places unknown—anywhere where she could get lost.

Behind her Sam bobbed through the crowds, still following her for whatever inane purpose, unable to do the right thing and just get lost. And that left Gaia with only one option. To get *herself* lost. If there was one thing Chinatown was perfect for, it was that.

Once again she broke into an angry sprint, her feet pelting the asphalt as she crossed Canal and swung down Mott Street. The Mandarin alphabet thickened on street signs, snaking up above noodle shop facades. She sped past families emerging from dim sum lunches, tiny stores crammed full of vases and silk pajamas, grocers selling fruits and fish. She didn't stop to see any of it. Nope. She didn't care what she saw. She didn't care, period. Because Sam evidently didn't care. About her or about anything—

"Gaia!" he shouted.

So why is he still chasing me?

His anger stopped her. She spun around to face him. What right did *he* have to sound so pissed?

"Why is it that your life can be one big secret, but I can't even keep just a little part of mine to myself?" Sam gasped, doubling over as he staggered to close the gap between them. "Don't tell me I know everything about you. I've had to knock down a lot of doors to get even the little information you've given me about your life."

Gaia bit the inside of her cheek. Slight point there. But she was changing. "Let's back up. You haven't exactly been one big open book since I've met you.

There's the small fact that you slept with my foster mother. . . ." She broke off, instantly regretting the words. Sam's face was whitewashed in pain, his mouth open like a wound. They'd made a pact to never mention that incident again. Gaia had broken her promise. She'd made a mistake. Especially since Sam hadn't even known who Ella was—

"Yo, Sam Moon!"

A jovial voice tore into the thickening silence.

Gaia turned to see a tall guy with dark hair and NYU sweats jog toward them.

"Josh," Sam hissed. He bristled, then backed away. Gaia glanced at him, puzzled. "It's my—my RA," he stammered. His eyes were wide. If he was still angry about the Ella comment, he didn't show it. There was no mistaking the look in his eye: It was fear. But why would he be scared of his RA? Anyway, wasn't Josh supposed to be Sam's new pal? She remembered Sam talking about him recently. . . .

"What's up?" Josh asked casually, glancing between the two of them. "You must be the lovely Gaia. Heard so much about you."

Gaia's eyes narrowed. *The lovely Gaia.* Well, she could see why Sam didn't like him anymore. His slick, oily, confident manner definitely rubbed her the wrong way, too. In fact, he looked like any number of annoying, handsome jocks who breezed through life—never struggling, never

113

suffering. But he certainly didn't come across as anyone to *fear*. Just someone to avoid.

Gaia opened her mouth to reply—but Sam caught her off guard, grabbing her arm. "We have to get going," he mumbled, half shoving Gaia down the street.

She frowned. "Hey—"

"There's no need to be rude, Sammy," Josh shouted after them.

Sammy?

Gaia shook loose of Sam's grasp, then glanced between the two of them.

There was a weird dynamic here, one she couldn't understand. Who on earth called Sam "Sammy"? But neither of them spoke for a moment. Sam was glaring at Josh. Gaia had never seen him so flustered.

"So you two are just hanging out in Chinatown, huh?" Josh asked, oozing his macho frat boy version of charm. "Just sight-seeing?"

"What do you want?" Sam spat. His voice was trembling.

Josh clucked his tongue. "You shouldn't be down here. You shouldn't be hanging out with Gaia." He flashed her a phony smile. "Nothing personal toward you, but Sammy knows he shouldn't be hanging out with you." He turned to Sam again, his smile vanishing. "You've got another test coming up, Sam. I know you don't want to fail."

"Another. . . test?" Gaia asked, completely bewildered now. That was news to her.

"I'm just going to take her home," Sam whispered.

"Good idea." Josh's eyes flashed to Gaia. "Well, I'll tell you, Gaia, I have noticed that Sam's been pretty tense lately, and I just keep trying to tell him to relax. Like I always say, things could be worse. Things could be much, much worse. You know what I mean, don't you, Gaia? Don't you ever just sit and contemplate how much worse your life could be—"

"We have to go!" Sam spat. He grabbed Gaia's arm again, dragging her down the street.

This time Gaia was too shocked to resist. Their rapport made absolutely no sense. As far as Gaia could tell, Josh was just an oaf with a penchant for spouting clichés. So why was Sam acting so weird?

"See you back at the dorm," Josh called. "And nice to meet you, Gaia. Hope I see *you* again real soon. . . ." His voice finally faded into the distance.

"What was that about?" Gaia hissed in Sam's ear.

He just shook his head, his face an unreadable mask.

"Nothing to do with us, huh?" Gaia asked. With a savage twist she pulled her arm free of Sam's grip. Ashen faced, he opened his mouth, apparently searching for the right words to say. As if there could be any. Too late. Gaia turned, and this time she really sprinted. Sam would never catch up to her

115

now—not if she put her mind to it, and that was exactly how it should be.

She'd had enough of the boyfriend-girlfriend thing for one day.

LOKI HAD SEEN SOME UGLY FACES

in his time. But every time that prison guard slid open the window of his cell door, he still couldn't help but gasp at the sheer hideousness of her features. That drooping, useless eye. And the black-and-yellow highlights of her teeth—she grinned each and every time she provided his meals—made  the virtually indigestible food even less appetizing. Worst of all were her bulbous cheeks, which seemed to fill every corner of the rather large window. . . . She was just repellent.

He made a mental note never to use her again once she'd completed this job for him.

"Lunch!" she announced with a primitive grunt. For what seemed like the thousandth time, she slid a tray through the midlevel slot in the door.

Loki grabbed his meal and immediately searched under the paper plate for his delivery. The moment his fingertips made contact with the flattened shrink-wrapped package, a smile overtook his stern expression. It was his first smile in days. And from this moment on, it certainly would not be his last. Loki peeled the package from under the tray and punctured the shrink-wrap, taking a nice long whiff.

Ahhh. Nothing like the scent of fresh laundry.

He made a mental note to have his entire wardrobe laundered for his return home. Which, thankfully, would be in just a few more days. The preparations had taken a tad longer than he'd predicted, but at last events were falling into place, and the plan was back on schedule.

Loki pranced back to his bed (there was room for about two steps of prancing in his claustrophobic cell) and placed the package under his mattress, humming the "Ode to Joy" from Beethoven's Ninth. Yes, it had become overexposed and bourgeois, but it seemed appropriate for the moment. He could feel the tide was turning back in his favor.

Permanently.

Freedom was just days away. Dinner at Compagno's, a comfortable bed, tailored shirts, and best of all. . . a brand-new daughter.

GAIA MOVED THROUGH THE CHILLY

darkness, a light rain sprinkling softly around her. It had been a long time since she'd done this—since she'd roamed the streets at night, looking for action. She crossed Little West Twelfth

Big Sugar-Coated Lie

Street for the second time already, staring into silent storefronts up and down dark alleys that glistened slick and empty.

Gaia's eyes raked right and left, desperate to lock onto something suspicious. Maybe a wife-beating alcoholic would materialize. Or a rapist. A bunch of looters. *Come on,* Gaia willed. It wasn't that late, only a little past ten. There had to be some thuggish activity so that she could jump in, kick some ass, and at least feel useful in the world. Anything beat trying to sleep with Sam's enigmatic, guilt-ridden face in her mind.

But there was simply nothing out here tonight. No one to punish. No one to save.

So much for the rough-and-ready Meat-Packing District. The place was deserted. She was alone in the softly falling rain.

Which meant she was forced to think about him again.

Beautiful Sam Moon.

118

I don't understand it, Sam, she called silently to him. *After all the shit we came through to get here. Why are you doing this?* True, Gaia was inexperienced with relationships. Meaning that she had no experience whatsoever. But somehow she had the feeling that even if she were a craggy old veteran of love— even if she were some kind of love guru, the love *doctor*—she'd still have no idea why Sam was being so distant.

It was so horribly twisted, in a way: She had returned from Paris as the "new" Gaia. But while she'd been away, the "old" Sam picked up and split.

She shook her head, glaring at the bleak cityscape. A couple of roundhouse kicks was all she wanted. Was that too much for a girl to ask?

Apparently, yes.

Her thoughts raced, scurrying across her mind like the rats that darted in and out of the neighborhood gutters. What was Sam keeping from her? What was really behind his half-baked attempt to placate her by insisting that there was nothing wrong between them? Why was Sam so damn nervous around her? It was so unlike him—or at least, who she *thought* he was. . . . Maybe it *was* just the pressure at school. Like Josh had suggested. Yeah, right. Bullshit. Sam had always managed to pick up his grades, no matter how fast and far he'd fallen. He was an ace student.

Maybe it was some kind of family thing?

No. He would have shared that with Gaia. At least, she thought he would.

An electric tingle fizzled in her veins. There was nothing to be scared of, obviously. Nothing around here, anyway. Even the meekest person in the world would probably feel comfortable in this spot. Just a little weird. No. . . but Gaia knew why she was feeling that sensation that always came instead of fear. It was because she was just circling around the obvious possibility.

Sam had finally spent enough time with her to know that he didn't love her.

No. It's not that simple. Sam loves you. He loves you, and you love him. But for whatever reason, you just can't stand to be around each other right now.

Strange. Before they'd even met, before they'd exchanged a single word, Gaia had thought about being with him all the time. Now that they were going out, being together was an impossibility. Yes, Camus was definitely right. Life was absurd.

Gaia walked east into the wind. The rain was coming down in sheets now. She felt exposed. As if people were staring at her from blackened windows. Only one person aside from Sam could make her feel better. . . but Ed had shut her off, too. He wasn't answering her calls; he wasn't replying to her e-mails.

That left her father. But did she really want to open up to him about her boyfriend problems? No. She'd done that once. It was enough. Anyway, he was having a drink with George Niven and would be home within the hour—and if she tried to get in touch with him anytime before then, he would probably have a panic attack. He thought she was home right now, after all.

Probably just as well. Perhaps she shouldn't share her problems with her dad or anyone else. Lately, sharing hadn't gotten her too far.

From Ed Fargo's Trash Mail Folder

To: gaia13@alloymail.com
From: shred@alloymail.com
Re: . . .—fargo. .—. . please. .—come. . .—in. . -.

G:

   I want to talk to you, too. I know I've been distant lately, but I have a very good reason, and it has to do with Heather. I've kept this to myself because I didn't want you to judge her too harshly re something v. important that I can't discuss in e-waves.

   Need to talk in person, urgently. I have to run this by you. You're the only one I trust.

   I have some exciting news, too.

Ed

From Ed Fargo's Sent Mail Folder

To: Gaia13@alloymail.com
From: shred@alloymail.com
Re: . . .—fargo. .—. . please. .—come. . .—in. . .—.

G:

Sorry I didn't reply sooner, but I've been busy. I got your phone message, too, but haven't had a chance to call back. Primarily because I am a lame ass. And in keeping with my current lame-ass status, no, I can't hook up tomorrow. I have a family thing.

Then I'll be attending the convention for lame asses. . . .

But in the meantime. . .

"Stay alive! No matter what occurs! I WILL CALL YOU!"

—A little Daniel Day Lewis from *Last of the Mohicans.*

Are my movie references getting too obscure? Yeah, I think so, too.

See you at school.

Ed

I think my daughter is withdraw-
ing from me. Tonight my meeting
ran late with George. He leaves
for Washington, D.C., tomorrow
morning, and there are concerns
about Loki that require our
fullest attention. When I came
home just before midnight, I
looked in on Gaia, worried that
she was still up, concerned that
I was not yet back. She lay
still, pretending to be asleep.
Everything was perfect: the even
rise and fall of her lungs, the
relaxed eyelids—except that I
knew she was faking it. Years of
experience has taught me the difference between sleep and a fac-
simile, no matter how good.

But why would Gaia pretend
with me?

Perhaps it is to be expected,
these moments where Gaia sees fit
to screen herself. I suppose I
had naively hoped for the impossible: that once Gaia and I were
reunited, she would forget about
the separation I had forced her

to endure for so long. Yet there is no denying that I put my daughter through years of bitterness that no amount of explaining can melt away.

The poor girl. I worry so for her happiness. And my work pressures are building. The agency has long since abandoned their lenient attitude. I won't have limitless time on my side. And the agency's impatience will affect my daughter. Not just her happiness, but most important, her safety. Gaia's protection is all that counts.

Sometimes it amazes me that after all I have seen and known, I still have the capacity for simplistic optimism. I still want to believe that Gaia could somehow forget everything that's happened between us, to trust me and open up to me without hesitation. As if that could make the world stop turning and grant me a reprieve from reality.

I stared at Gaia tonight,

watched her pretend to sleep, remembering all the times I sat beside her bed when she was just a little girl and watched her sleep and dream. Happy dreams, her small mouth curling in a sleepy smile. But she is no longer a little girl, though it is hard for me to accept that she is almost a woman. She is navigating her way through the world. And tonight she did not sleep. She just lay there, perhaps sensing my thoughts, my doubts, and my fears.

She has great instincts, Gaia. The road is still treacherous ahead of us, and sooner or later there will be more difficult choices to face. It is only a matter of time.

She wondered
why she had to
torture herself
with a visual
complete
representation
of how **sucker**
her reality was
swirling down
the drain.

"LOSING YOUR EDGE. BIG TIME."

A Metaphor for Life

Renny smiled and nudged one of Gaia's pawns off the board with his bishop in one graceful swipe.

Renny. He had the face of an angel, eyes like two big, chocolate brown M&M's. A scrawny body swimming somewhere underneath his trying-too-hard Fubu jeans. He could also make you look stupid if you weren't careful. Like now. It was the second time in a week that an opponent had caught Gaia completely off guard. But she couldn't help it. She was too caught up in her own funk. Half miserable and tired from her lonely night in the Meat-Packing District, looking for God knows what. And half hopeful that the sun had cracked through her thundercloud. That her father's gooey French toast breakfast signaled that all was not lost in the world.

It was more than homemade French toast with an overload of Aunt Jemima, though. Her father had asked Gaia to invite Sam out to dinner with them for tomorrow night. He said it could be their very first dinner party. And he wanted to meet Ed, too.

Though Gaia had woken up ready to nail her fist through the wall, her father's dinner party idea had disarmed her.

Touched her. For a while it had seemed like he might always have to lie low and not be a part of her life in the way that other dads could be, meeting boyfriends and best friends. Losing the dark glasses.

Because now that her father had offered, it could only mean that he was here to stay—and the secrecy that cloaked his life was finally on its way out the door.

Gaia smiled as happy images drifted through her mind. Her dad, challenging Sam to a chess match. Talking films with Ed.

"Excuse me?" Renny asked. "You playing or not?"

"I'm in recovery," Gaia said as she made her move.

Renny raised an eyebrow. But he couldn't know what her plan was. It was still several moves away from completion, an attack on Renny's castled king through the bishop sacrifice at h7. And that little thirteen-year-old punk sitting across from her, whom she also grudgingly happened to adore, was about to get his ass whipped sorry. Because Gaia was hanging on to the good vibes produced by her dad's interest in Sam and Ed. Her chess game was taking a turn for the better, as was her life. Wasn't that what people said about chess, anyway? That it was just a metaphor for life? *On the up. . .*

. . . and down.

A thought occurred to her.

Sam and Ed would probably be about as interested

in meeting Gaia Moore's dad as they were in hanging out with Gaia Moore.

"Don't you think it sucks that Kasparov lost the world championship to Vladimir Kramnik?" Renny asked. He nudged a piece forward, then folded his hands in a steeple.

"Yeah. No. Haven't really thought about it," Gaia muttered sulkily. She chewed on her thumbnail as she stared at the board and she realized she'd been over-hasty and overconfident in her play. Renny had pre-empted her next move. He knew exactly what she was up to—and why shouldn't he? This was shoddy strategy on her part. Way beneath her level.

"Sneaky does it." Renny grinned. With a swift move he pushed Gaia's game in tight after she'd been forced to change her play. No more fun strategies now. It would be defenses only, no hope of winning. Just a long drawn-out claustrophobic march toward inevitable doom. Gaia smirked. Chess really was a metaphor for life. Better to just die fast. Her face creased into a mask of resignation as she appraised the chessboard. She wondered why she had to torture herself with a visual representation of how her reality was swirling down the drain. Overconfidence leads to vulnerability leads to...

"Checkmate."

Gaia forked over a twenty, clipped Renny lightly on the side of his head, and then stood up. "Bite me," she said with a smile, jamming her fingers into a pair of ratty brown fingerless gloves.

"Love to," Renny replied.

Gaia shuffled off through the park toward LaGuardia Place. Only one thing could alleviate the status quo: a biggie box of Good & Plenty. Gaia had become addicted to the stuff in the last few days. The chewy pink and white candies gave her an excellent, vivifying sugar hit—even better than Krispy Kreme doughnuts. Besides, there was no reason to feel self-conscious about the black licorice stain on her teeth. It wasn't like she needed to look kissable.

"Gaia!"

Except. . .

The voice was as familiar as the footsteps drawing near. Why couldn't Sam find another park? She glanced up at him. There was a better question, actually: Why the hell did those windswept curls still have the lame effect of intoxicating her—even as she felt a knife plunging through her heart? A knife that twisted on sight of Sam's tentative smile?

"Hey," he offered.

Gaia didn't answer.

"I never really understood the point of fingerless gloves," Sam murmured. "I mean, it's the extremities of the fingers that feel the cold most, right? So insulating everything except for the tips will only make them feel worse."

"If you say so." Gaia stepped away from him. What was this? Med school moments? If he wanted to make small talk, he was even more of a coward than she'd given him credit for.

"No. Gaia, wait." Sam reached for her arm. "I came here to find you. I've been crazy knowing how much I upset you. I'm so sorry about yesterday."

I'll bet. But Gaia didn't move. She waited, even though she knew she shouldn't give him the chance to explain himself. But what did she have to lose that she hadn't already lost? Pride had long since been tossed out the door. She'd left it on Canal Street, in fact. It was probably on its way to China by now.

"I can't tell you what's happening right now, but I swear, Gaia, this is not about us. I need you. I—"

Sam broke off. Gaia turned to him. She shivered momentarily, struck by how ghastly he actually looked up close. His eyes were bloodshot, filled with nervous energy and the kind of glazed look that only comes from not sleeping. His cheekbones protruded, too, underscored by bruiselike shadows. When had he gotten so gaunt?

"What's happening to you?" Gaia whispered softly, forgetting herself, suspended by Sam's obvious distress. She saw it in his face again—the same emotion she'd seen on Mott Street. Fear. For some twisted reason, the inability to feel fear herself only made her hyperaware of its presence in others. And then she felt like kicking herself. Seeing Sam so spooked, she suddenly felt like she'd been walking around in a blind stupor for the past week, if not longer.

"You have to know you can trust me." Sam's voice was low and strong. "And I know you're worried, but you have to believe I've got this covered. But if you leave me, Gaia, I—"

She threw her arms around him, cutting off his speech, cutting off the need for speech itself. She felt absurd doing so, but it was the only option left. She was worn out from playing hardball. Whatever Sam was going through, he needed her support, not her anger or interference. And if he needed her to trust him and keep out—then hard as it was going to be, she had to give it a shot.

Or something like that.

Gaia tightened her arms around him, wondering if she'd just made a huge mistake in this single act. But it was a bit late to backtrack. And there were worse things to be than a complete sucker. A complete cynic, for one. Of course, that was something the old Gaia would never cop to. But this was the new Gaia, for better or worse.

"This is just a temporary thing that I have to get through," Sam whispered into Gaia's hair. "And when it's over, I promise there won't be any more secrets. Ever."

"Okay," Gaia whispered. She stepped away from him. "But only if you do something for me. It's going to be difficult. Maybe even painful."

"What?" Sam asked, edgy.

"Have dinner with me and my dad. Tomorrow night."

He blinked. "That's it?"

"That's it," Gaia said. She could feel a smile curling on her lips.

Sam laughed, heaving a sigh of relief. "Of—of course," he stammered. "I'd love to have dinner with you and your dad."

Gaia tilted her head to kiss him. "Swear you won't let me down," she demanded, staring into his eyes. "Don't screw me over here, Sam."

"I swear," Sam murmured. Gaia felt a flare of warmth somewhere deep inside her chest. Oddly enough, she felt it on her head, too.

Something warm and oozing and wet. She reached up and touched it.

"Crap!" Gaia cried. Her face wrinkled. Her hand came back dripping with a runny, chalky substance. It smelled like ammonia. "A pigeon just shat on my head!" She glanced up, searching the gray skies, but the offending bird had fled.

Sam smiled and put a hand to Gaia's cheek. "That's good luck."

"No, it's not. If bird shit lands on your *shoulder*, it's good luck." Gaia fumbled in her messenger bag for a shred of Kleenex she'd once spotted lurking inside. "I think on the head is a bad omen."

Sam didn't say anything. And that was good. Because in those kinds of situations, it was best to keep one's mouth shut.

"I'M BORED," HEATHER COMPLAINED, Wide Open

sitting against the wall at the back of Ed's bed.

Ed rolled his eyes and looked back at her from the front of the bed. That was no surprise. Nor was it a huge surprise that she was picking her nails. Every little thing she did tonight seemed to be more irritating than the last.

"Just try to get into this." Ed groaned. "It's *The Last of the Mohicans*. It's a totally famous old book, and this is a Michael Mann classic."

Heather snorted, without even bothering to look up at him. "Why is that guy always running up a mountain with no shirt on?"

"He's an Indian. He's trying to save his people, for God's sake. Watch the movie."

"Whatever." Heather groaned, too. "I *am* watching the movie."

Ed turned back to the screen, scowling. Actually, that was the problem. They *were* watching the movie—instead of using it as a background to drown out the sounds of making out, as was tradition. He tried desperately to think of ways to cut through this endless tension. If he didn't tell her how truly pissed he was, he was likely to explode.

And if you really didn't want to talk to her, you wouldn't have invited her over.

True. There was no arguing with himself. He always lost. Anyway, he didn't enjoy the fact that things were so awful between them. Because he was positive that there was a huge part of Heather that wasn't about money at all. That was the Heather he'd known before—the Heather he'd fallen in love with years ago, before the accident. He just had to find her inside *this* Heather. He just had to dig a little.

"Intermission?" Ed asked.

Heather nodded curtly.

He pressed pause, then reached over to the bars above his bed and hoisted himself into the air. "And now ye shall be entertained by the smooth orthopedic maneuvers of Shred Fargo, all the way from his wheelchair. . . and into your heart!"

Heather smiled wanly. At least she'd stopped picking her nails. If he could show her the progress he'd made, then maybe she would perk up. After all, she hadn't actually seen what he could do. Maybe she would be more enthusiastic after the show. And maybe then they would cut through this impasse in their relationship—blow everything wide open so they could put it all back together piece by piece. Get back on track.

"Watch," he instructed.

Slowly Ed pulled himself up on the walking bars, ramrod straight. Then gently he lowered himself, using his arm muscles to keep himself in the air. *Focus*, he ordered himself—imagining Brian there by his side, screaming and blasting music. Ed's biceps bulged with the pressure. He looked down, watching as his feet floated toward the floor. Then touched the floor. Biting his lip in concentration, Ed forced his fingers away from the bar, transferring weight from his upper body to his legs in a mental leap of faith.

Standing.

One second. . . two. . . three—

"What are you doing?" Heather shrieked.

"What does it look like I'm doing?" Ed croaked. He glanced at her with a red-faced grin, his entire body shaking from the strain. "I'm standing, that's what I'm—"

"Well, *stop it!*" Heather jumped off the bed. Her eyes were wide, her forehead creased. She ran to Ed's door and flipped the latch to lock it. "Are you crazy?" she hissed, enraged. "Your folks might see you."

"Heather." Ed emphasized each syllable of her

name. His concentration was beginning to wane. The pain in his legs was swiftly turning to torture. He would have to sit in a second or two. But not yet. Not until she understood the magnitude of this event. "I'm standing on my. . . own. . . two. . . feet," he choked out, quavering.

"Shhh. Ed." She jerked a thumb at the door. "Someone might hear you."

"Jesus!" Ed glared at her. "I'm standing, Heather!"

"I *see* that," she hissed back. "Now, would you please sit down?"

All at once his legs gave out on him. He collapsed to his bed. Rage swept through his body, complementing the pain. "You don't want me to walk," he growled, his throat burning. "Or maybe you just don't give a shit either way. As long as you get your money."

Heather flinched as if she'd been struck. "How can you say that?" she shot back. "Of course I want you to walk again."

"Well, you have a strange way of showing it." Sickened, Ed buried his face in his pillows, his eyes glazing over with tears. He didn't want to look at Heather anymore. He couldn't stand the sight of her—that corrupted beauty.

"Have you ever thought that maybe I'm containing my enthusiasm because I don't want you to get your hopes up?" Heather asked. Her voice was shaking. She must be crying, too. He heard her gathering her belongings. "The doctors said that the success isn't guaranteed. Remember?"

Ed remembered. How could he not remember? But maybe she was just saying that because she didn't *want* the operation to be a success. Maybe it was true: All she cared about was getting that money. If Ed couldn't walk, she'd be a rich woman.

"I need to be cautious for you, Ed," Heather continued, her voice choked with tears. "I thought one of us. . . oh, what's the use. Enjoy the movie, Ed. You know, maybe you should invite Gaia Moore over here to watch it with you. You always believe the best of her and the worst of me, anyway."

Heather slammed the door, and Ed could hear her muffled sobs as she stomped down the hall.

Good. He was glad she was upset. She deserved to have her own selfishness flung back in her face. No one ever gave Heather any shit, and maybe that's why she'd become so spoiled and self-absorbed. Ed had done the right thing.

Sure, you did.

Show Time

"WE NEED TO TALK," SAM STATED bluntly.

He stood in the doorway of Josh's room. Josh

lay on his bed—*Mike's bed*—looking as relaxed as ever, in that same sweat suit, that same smile on his face. Sam began to seriously consider the possibility that Josh wasn't human. He never changed. Never, no matter what time of day or night. He was always well rested. Smug. Confident. Maybe he was some kind of demon, or vampire, or robot—

"What's up?" Josh asked, plumping the pillow behind his head.

For about the thousandth time in the last twenty-four hours, Sam had a vivid fantasy of killing him. But that wouldn't solve anything.

"I'm not going to do it anymore," Sam said. His extremities tingled with anxiety, but he kept his face blank.

"Do what?" Josh asked, almost sleepily.

"I swear to God, Josh, I'll—"

"You'll what?" Josh interrupted. His blue eyes clouded. "You've gotten a taste of what you're dealing with here, Sammy. Just a taste. So you know that you're in absolutely no position to make demands." His voice softened. "Don't screw yourself *now*. Not when you're so close."

Sam blinked, fighting to ignore the chill that enveloped his body. "Close to *what?*" he asked.

Josh laughed. "Oh, no. I am *not* going to spoil the surprise."

140

Sam suddenly realized his fists were clenched so tightly that he was digging his nails into the palms of his hands. Never before had he felt so completely out of control, so powerless. He didn't know what he'd intended to accomplish by confronting Josh like this. But he hadn't been thinking; his rage over the way Josh had acted around Gaia annihilated every rational impulse. Still, he knew better than to do something rash. Someone could be watching them right now. Someone was probably snapping pictures of every gesture, recording every word.

"I'm not going to do it anymore," Sam heard himself whisper. "I *can't.* Just tell me who you're working for, Josh. Let me talk to them."

For a moment Josh just stared at him. "You're losing it, buddy." He lay back down on his bed, then grabbed a bottle of spring water from his nightstand and tossed it to Sam. "Have some water. You look like you could use some. It's important to stay healthy, after all. It's almost show time."

Show time? The words snaked down Sam's spine. Another stupid joke. . . but there was cold finality in it. And of course, he didn't have a clue what Josh was talking about. It was just one more huge mystery that involved Sam's life—and for all he knew, his death. But as he hurled the bottle of water against the wall, he realized he didn't want to know what it meant.

Ours is not to reason why; ours is but to do and die. . . .

To: J
From: L
Date: February 16
File: 001
Subject: Dinner party

Costume received. Confirm that guest will be attending. Please inform upon delivery of party favors.

To: L
From: J
Date: February 16
File: 001
Subject: Dinner party

Guest is confirmed. Impressive work. Truly uncanny. Party favor status to follow.

Love

means implicit, unconditional trust in the person you're with. When they ask for space or tell you they need to sort something out by themselves, something they can't share with you, you oblige them. You don't second-guess.

Like hell, you don't.

I gave Sam the benefit of the doubt today, but I've spent every moment since then second guessing my decision. Part of me knows I need to support Sam. But the other part thinks I'm setting myself up for disaster. Let's face it, "asking for space" is just a euphemism for deception. Sam and I swore we would have an honest relationship after all the crap that preceded it. But we've barely even begun, and this is where we are.

Still, if I can't trust Sam to know when to spill and when to keep silent, what does that say about my ability to love him?

But I do love him. I want to help him.

Major dilemma.

So tonight, after driving
myself insane for so long, I came
up with the only rational solution: I took my biggie box of
Good & Plenty and shook it up so
that all the pinks and whites
were mixed nicely. Then I decided
white was the color of trust and
love and all things good. And
pink was the color of deception
and danger and all things bad,
like the plus sign on pregnancy
tests. I've seen a lot of pink on
the FOHs recently, so the desig-
nation of color significance was
not arbitrary.

And then I fumbled in the box
precisely three times, three
being the number of sugars I take
in my coffee.

I drew three candies. If it
turned out that there were more
whites than pinks, then I'd trust
Sam and stick to my promise not
to pry. If pink came out on top,
then I'd do some snooping.

Three whites.

Love means implicit, unconditional trust in. . . yeah, well,
whatever.

Best just not to think about
Sam. But Ed is a different story,
and I don't need candy to help me
out with my game plan there. True
friendship is unconditional, and
Ed and I have always been honest
with each other. But now he's
just straight pissing me off.
It's like he wants me to drop him
and quit trying.

This reminds me of Mary Moss
and of how close I came to losing
her friendship before it even
began. I even walked away. But
luckily Mary just forced herself
back into my life, and for that I
will always be grateful. I can't
let Ed slip away like that. And
if that means forcing myself back
in, then so be it. It's not like
I've ever been averse to using
force where necessary.

How can a person know when it's the right time to give up on something or someone? Where is the cutoff point, the moment you finally realize there's too much water under the bridge and the bridge itself is officially being burned?

Here's a better question: How much is love worth?

A guy can really go crazy on that one. I'm of the opinion that it's impossible to assign a monetary value to love, but it seems like I might be alone there. So I've been trying to work it out. There's no material difference between $999,999 and $1 million, or between $26 million and $25,999,999. Yet everyone has to have a limit, that figure where they would trade money for the person they love. "I'd do it for a billion, but not a dollar less." Sure, a cutoff point in this game of numbers always has to be random and artificial. But that's the nature of the game.

And when you really think about it, in the end, what you basically have is someone willing to sell out the person they love for one measly buck.

I wonder if Heather has played this game.

I know I shouldn't cast her as some mercenary. The situation is complicated. But I can't ignore the fact that she just isn't there for me now. Not in the way that counts. I need encouragement, not negativity, and even if—best-case scenario—she's holding back her support because she doesn't want to get my hopes up, she's still holding back.

Gaia would be elated for me if she knew, no matter what her problems. But Heather's too caught up in her own world. Instead she's forcing my hand, forcing me to lie and stay squarely in the wheelchair. Which begs another question: If Heather is with me for the money, then what does that say about me if

I'm willing to give it to her?

Am I buying her love? Am I just as low?

Either way, there's a lot wrong with this picture.

You know, the wheelchair has always been a hindrance, limiting my mobility. But it's never felt like a trap. Until now. Literally and figuratively stuck, that's where I am. And here's the final irony: I could just walk away, probably in more ways than one. So why don't I? Because I can't help hearing Heather's words: that I always think the worst of her.

Heather, give me a reason to think the best of you. I'm waiting to hear it. Don't worry. I'm not going anywhere.

Sam went cold.
He was over
the edge now,
well and
truly. He **jokes**
was hearing **about**
wheelchairs
voices,
coming out
of the wall.

"SORRY!" GAIA PANTED, SPRINTING
down the sidewalk. She'd almost flattened a tiny, bespectacled old crone
in a polka-dotted blouse. The woman
had appeared out of nowhere. Like a
thousand other people. The streets of
Greenwich Village were just too
damn crowded in the morning.

Right-of-way

"Jesus! Watch where you're going, bitch!"

Gaia laughed as she flew toward the drab red pile
of bricks that was the Village School, amazed at the
words falling from such prim and wizened lips.
Amazed, yet not. That was New York. Nobody—not
even little blue-haired ladies—stood on ceremony for
anyone. *And just when I was beginning to feel bad for
almost knocking down a sweet little old lady. . .* lesson
two about New York: What you saw was never what
you got.

In spite of all her problems and woes, Gaia actually
felt halfway decent today. Sure, she'd overslept. But
that was par for the course. At least she was going to
school. Maybe she was just optimistic because it was
Friday. Tonight was the dinner with Sam and her dad.
Tonight she would set things straight,
get to the bottom of whatever it was that
was torturing her boyfriend. Tonight all
would be made well.

They had reservations at Le Jardin. She had even

found a half-decent dress to wear, a slim-fitting black number that her father had bought for her in Paris and that she could just tolerate seeing herself in. On second thought, maybe she should just wear jeans, be her usual mangy self. After all, the ratty girl was the one Sam had fallen for. . . .

She drew in a deep breath as she clattered up the school stairs and burst through the big double doors. The only problem, of course, was that Ed wouldn't be there. She hadn't even had a chance to talk to him about it. But maybe she should just tackle one problem at a time. After she'd settled with Sam, she would settle with Ed. Things were almost back to normal with them, anyway. *Almost* being the key word—

Speak of the devil.

There was a flash of metal at her side, followed by the sound of skidding. Ed's wheelchair swerved in front of her, momentarily cutting her off. She had to laugh. She was having major pedestrian traffic problems today.

"Goddamn paraplegics think they got the right-of-way," she quipped.

Ed screeched to a stop. He whirled and glared at her. "You know, I'm really looking forward to the day when I don't have to put up with shit like that anymore," he spat.

Time seemed to freeze.

Gaia gaped at him. *Wait a second.* Had she just

been beamed into some alternate universe? Jokes about wheelchairs were kosher. Calling a spade a spade was how Gaia and Ed had always operated. That was part of the reason they'd become friends in the first place. It was the no-bullshit, no-euphemism fulcrum around which their entire friendship turned. She'd meant the remark as an icebreaker, as a way of saying that everything was still cool between them.

"Uh. . . sorry," she mumbled, not knowing how to react—suddenly wishing she could run outside and come back in all over again, start the school day from scratch. But she couldn't help but be annoyed, too. How the hell was she supposed to know that Ed had abruptly developed a sensitive streak?

"No, it's cool," Ed muttered, his face unreadable, a mix of emotions that Gaia couldn't translate. "I just meant that I didn't feel like. . . that I was sick of. . . look, just ignore me, okay? Things'll be better once. . . Forget it."

"Once what?" Gaia prompted, baffled.

He shook his head. "Forget it."

All at once Gaia was angry. She was sick of this—sick of sweating through people's odd moods and silences. You'd think between Ed and Sam, one of them might give the cryptology a rest. . . . But then, apparently, you'd have to think again. She scrutinized Ed's face as if she were deciphering a map. Clues to some inner turmoil were there, all right. But they pointed at nothing concrete. Or at too many things. There was apology in there. And worry. But something else, too. Something like anxiety but with more of a kick in it. Excitement?

"Things'll be better once. . ."

Gaia's lips tightened. Ed was beginning to sound a hell of a lot like Sam. Yes, it was definitely a good thing that Ed wasn't coming to the dinner tonight. Dealing with one secretive jerk at a time was about all she could handle.

"PLEASE STAND CLEAR OF THE *closing doors."*

Veiny Hands

Sam gripped the metal pole as the subway doors pinged shut, watching as the Thirty-fourth Street station receded from view. Warily his eyes flicked across the train compartment. He felt like he'd swallowed a steel rod: His stomach was cold and uncomfortable, and he wasn't hungry, even though he'd barely eaten all day. Once again he was looking for something. Someone. Only he didn't have even the vaguest idea who that person was. Which meant it could be anyone.

Anybody. Everybody.

Sam shivered. His mind seemed to race the train itself, one suspicion tumbling over the next as he recast the sequence of events that had led him to this moment.

Point of origination: Mike's death. *No, Ella.* Or maybe before that. . .

One more stop to go: Grand Central Station. But the journey through the black tunnel seemed interminable. The fluorescent lighting hurt Sam's eyes. He was bone tired, so tired that his body felt wired into overdrive, every cell screaming and throbbing. Sleep was no longer an option. Not since the nightmares, and not since Sam had known for sure that someone was watching him. Beyond the guys Gaia had found trying to break into his room. Beyond a doubt.

He'd felt it in the library. He'd felt it walking home after talking with Gaia in the park. Unseen eyes. Unseen, all-seeing eyes. Sam watched the floor. Anything to avoid looking at the people around him. They could all be with. . . *them.* The sullen Latino guy hiding behind a paperback in the corner. The upscale exec with her cat-frame glasses and the pencil at her lip. She could easily just be in "work" disguise. He thought he might truly lose it now, if he hadn't already. Paranoia. Sam would have laughed if he hadn't been thoroughly stripped of that ability.

154

He'd actually begun to feel paranoid about paranoia itself.

Chasing your own tail.

Suddenly Sam's forehead turned fiery hot. He'd heard that line very recently. Was it from his dreams? Hadn't someone said that to him while he lay in a diabetic slump on the cold, hard floors of some warehouse?

Or was that just another instance of paranoia feeding off itself?

The train jerked to a stop. Jesus. He hadn't even noticed he'd arrived.

The doors slid open, and Sam bolted straight for Grand Central terminal. Before exiting the turnstile, he stood for a moment leaning against a pillar, the white tile cooling off the skin of his cheek as he struggled to force his head clear. He had to keep it together. Focus on the positives: The police were no longer looking for him, and this was the last pickup.

So says Josh.

Sam laughed hollowly, tearing himself away from the pillar and moving between clouds of commuters and groups of tourists. What else did he have to go on but Josh's word? He had no choice but to believe Josh. None at all. As he reached the main concourse, he couldn't help but glance up at the famous ceiling: turquoise, decorated with the signs of the zodiac and twenty-five hundred stars in pinpricks of electric light. What he would give to be out in space right now, drifting, alone, far from this planet. . . a bittersweet ping of nostalgia shot through him. He'd seen this with his mother shortly after the renovation had been unveiled. They'd stopped for lunch at the Oyster Bar. . . a million lifetimes ago, yet so tantalizingly recent that he could almost taste it. . . .

Get a grip!

Sam turned his head away from the throng of passersby. He felt seasick. *Breathe.* Abruptly Sam stopped. He realized he'd found the designated spot: an anonymous pillar in a corner where the arteries of two tunnels bisected each other. He stood under the arch, searching the faces that flickered by. But no one paused. One minute slipped into the next. He faced the wall, sucked in air, and talked himself down. The last pickup. This would be the very last—

"Hellooo, Sam. . ."

Sam went cold. He was over the edge now, well and truly. He was hearing voices, coming out of the wall.

"Hello, Sam Moon."

That was it. Time to get out of here. Book himself into a lunatic hospital. A nervous breakdown, that was what he was having. . . voices in the wall. . . the insidious whispering. The hair on the back of his neck stood at attention. Flipping out, he was flipping out, losing the edge, losing the—

"I know you can hear me, Sam Moon."

He slipped down the cold pillar, shaking. And then he saw it. Him. A thin, spidery man diagonally opposite him, standing where the arch above them bisected another pillar. He smiled at Sam, turned, and whispered into the corner.

"Didn't I tell you that you could hear me?"

An acoustic effect. Some chance amplification of sound waves through the placement of tiled pillar and arch. That was all. His sanity was still intact. Well, maybe not intact... but he should be thankful for small favors. Stiffly Sam approached the man and without a word accepted a brown-paper-wrapped package from his veiny hands. The man smiled again, gave an impish salute, and walked away.

Manhattan Federal Prison

Sam read the instruction without expression, then opened his bag, the buzz of the Velcro like a chain saw to his hyperattuned ears. After tucking the package inside, he walked through the terminal's giant hall, craned his neck, and looked up at the stars.

Taurus, the bull. Aquarius, the water bearer.

But the vaulted ceiling's imagery didn't calm him. It only gave him pause to run the same conflicting ideas through his numb brain, to turn the dots of light into visual representations of his fears. *Enough.* Sam

157

continued walking—back through the drop zone, where three children now giggled and whispered into the corners of pillars. Apparently everyone knew this trick. Everyone but him.

He supposed he should feel used to being left in the dark by now.

INSULT ME ALREADY, GAIA DE-manded silently. *What are you waiting for?*

But Heather just stared straight through Gaia as if she were made of glass. "Have you seen Ed?" she asked in her new robo-voice, completely devoid of anything even vaguely approximating emotion.

"No," Gaia answered. Not since their early morning near collision, anyway. After Ed's fuzzy apology, he'd disappeared. And since Gaia didn't have a class with Ed until after lunch, she'd passed the time by carefully prepping the speech she would present to him. This time he wouldn't worm his way out of her questions. Once Gaia saw Ed again, she'd get the truth if it killed her. Or him.

"Look, I need to talk to him," Heather said, her

voice catching slightly. "So if you know where he is, I would appreciate your telling me."

"I thought he was with you," Gaia said. It was true. Gaia knew Ed had a free period. Since she hadn't seen him anywhere, she'd assumed he was off somewhere having a tête-à-tête with his girlfriend. . . .

Heather turned her back to Gaia and began furiously scribbling on a piece of paper. When she was done, she folded it, walked toward Ed's locker, and slipped it in through the crack in the locker door. Gaia shook her head as Heather disappeared down the corridor. *Your guess is as good as mine,* she said silently. Apparently for once both Gaia and Heather had the same ax to grind. Ed's mysterious behavior was getting to both of them. And now Ed's bizarre behavior spells had extended to include disappearance.

If Ed wasn't with Heather, then where was he?

Last Chance

"THANKS, MAN." SAM JUMPED UP from his desk and gratefully took the pile of experiment notes from Keon. At least he still had *one* friend. Or at least a guy who could stand in his doorway without cringing or asking him to commit a felony. "Did I miss anything?"

Keon shrugged. "Krause had us do more gravity experiments. Although it looks like you've been doing some of your own." He grinned, surveying the pile of clothes stacked on top of Sam's bed. "Nice tower. Is that a conceptual art piece or something?"

Sam managed a tired smile. "Somewhere in here is a clean shirt," he explained. "I'm having dinner with Gaia. And her father."

"Out of the frying pan and into the fire," Keon joked, leaning against the door frame. "From Heather straight to Gaia. You don't waste time, man."

"Mmmm." Sam hadn't really thought about that before. Nor did he want to think about it now. He had enough to feel anxious about. Like meeting Tom Moore. He began to rummage through the clothes for the button-down oxford he wanted to wear. This was a real chance to act *normal*. For Gaia. For her dad. He had to be willing to suspend all his haunting fears and suspicions. At least for one night.

"So you're meeting her father, huh?" Keon raised an eyebrow as Sam continued to search. "Scary."

"Maybe," Sam said. Or maybe not. He really didn't know what to expect. All he knew about Tom Moore was that he was capable of making Gaia either blissfully happy or totally miserable.

"I'd be careful with the guy if I were you," Keon

said. He removed his glasses and began to clean them with his sweatshirt.

Sam abruptly stopped tossing clothes around. "What do you mean?"

"Well." Keon looked up, still smiling, and put his glasses back on. "You're seeing the man's daughter, right? Ergo: he's not your number-one fan. Law of nature." He shrugged and turned to leave. "Good luck, Moon Man. Enjoy your dinner."

Sam just stood there as Keon disappeared down the hall. His pulse quickened.

Tom Moore. Not my number-one fan.

Whoever was orchestrating Sam's rather intricate and systematic torture would need a whole lot of resources at their disposal. They'd need surveillance equipment. They'd need contacts at the police department, contacts at the federal jail. They'd need to be watching Sam every minute of the day. Didn't the CIA fit every single aspect of that description?

His stomach squeezed.

Was all this madness the work of a demented and overly protective father?

No, no, no. He was going crazy again. His synapses were fried. He slowly walked into the suite's common room and sat down heavily on the couch. He needed to skip this mental road to nowhere. Suspecting Gaia's father was totally, royally out of line. Plain desperate.

But as Sam did his best to extricate himself from this particularly disturbing bout of paranoia, he felt a familiar tingling at the back of his neck. An unmistakable feeling that he couldn't deny.

He was being watched. Again.

Just because I can't see anyone doesn't mean no one's out there—

The phone rang in his room. He jumped up and dashed to pick it up, hoping it was Gaia. She could calm him. She could allay his fears.

"Hello?" he asked breathlessly.

"Moon. Josh here."

He bristled. Just his luck. "What do you want?"

"Hate to do this to you, but you gotta stay in tonight."

Sam's face darkened. He gripped the phone as if it were Josh's neck. "No way." The job was over. Josh had said so.

"I said no more deliveries," Josh mumbled. "I didn't say we wouldn't be having any—"

"I have a date tonight!" Sam screamed.

"With the TV," Josh interjected. "Sorry, buddy, but I can't let you go out. Someone might get hurt, you know?"

The color drained from Sam's face. "Why? Why are you—"

There was a click, and the line went dead.

Slowly Sam replaced the receiver, his throat tightening as he thought of Gaia. There was no way in hell she'd forgive him if he canceled this date. He knew very well this was a last-chance type of scenario. But if he didn't cancel? Josh wasn't bluffing when he said someone could get hurt. Somebody could do real damage to Gaia. And if there was even the slightest fraction of a chance that Gaia's well-being could somehow be connected to Josh's orders, then Sam had to take Josh seriously.

Sam swallowed and checked the time. She would be out of school and hanging in the park by now. He put on his leather jacket and switched off the iron.

He had places to be, hearts to break.

To: J
From: L
Date: February 17
File: 001
Subject: Dinner party

Party favors have been delivered. Guest is
confirmed. Costumes provided. All systems are go.
Enjoy.

Billy clubs
flew,
smacking
against raw

unexpected

flesh. Blood **rage**
spilled.
It was
glorious.

"DINNER!"

Loki was truly grateful that this would be the last time he'd have to look at that lazy-eyed prison guard through the window of his cell door. Yes. Thank the Lord in heaven. Not that Loki believed in any such supreme deity, but prison time—even so brief—brought odd changes to a man's thinking processes.

The Preparty

Thank God, indeed.

This would be the last rotting smile, the last primitive call to the troughs for the slop they dared to call food, the last hour of this gray claustrophobic purgatory.

The last supper.

He chuckled.

"Be sure and wipe your hands," the bloated guard suggested as she slid his dinner through the door slot.

"I always do," Loki replied. He grabbed his tray. Despite this woman's grotesque appearance, he had to admit that she was a diligent servant.

"Be *sure* and wipe your hands," she repeated, sliding the window shut.

Loki smiled wickedly and brought his tray to his bed, instantly tearing the plastic pouch that contained his utensils: a plastic fork and knife, a small napkin, and a prepackaged moist towelette. Only there was no moist towelette inside the pouch—but rather Loki's parting gifts for the entire cell block. One ultraslim book of five matches. One pouch of kerosene. A folded message no bigger than the missive in a Chinese fortune cookie.

Welcome to the dinner party. Let's start a fire!

Extreme Caution

"OUR REPORTS INDICATE THAT ALL is well. He's under complete, round-the-clock observation, and his appeal has been denied. We're on top of this."

Tom nodded back at his friend, George Niven—the man who'd cared for his daughter for five years, the man who had done so much for him and lost almost everything in return. Recently Tom had become extremely concerned about George. There was no doubt that Ella's death had taken its toll on him. George looked older, grayer, more haggard. He rarely smiled. Not that he would have any reason to smile. Tom couldn't even begin to fathom what it must feel to learn that your wife of five years was in fact an agent of Loki.

Still, sitting in this cozy bar in the early evening,

surrounded by civilians, Tom could almost feel. . . safe.

But safety was an illusion. "We're on top of this," George repeated reassuringly.

"I know." Tom sighed and took a long pull on his coffee. "But. . ."

"But you're still worried," George preempted, nodding sympathetically and signaling to the waitress to refill their coffee cups.

Tom raked a hand through his hair, his right knee jiggling under the table. He forced it to stop. This was a nervous tic, developed over the last few years—and nervous tics could mean the death of someone in his position. Why did he feel so on edge? Loki was incarcerated. His organization might still be floundering to survive— but the man himself was safely locked away in a maximum security facility. His minions were all headless chickens, staggering around without direction. Soon they would die—some figuratively, some literally. So *why* couldn't Tom stop worrying about his brother? Maybe because he knew Oliver just a little better than everyone else. No amount of surveillance could—

"Please, Tom. Try to relax."

"I can't help it," Tom murmured. "I just can't get over my fears that Gaia and I aren't safe. I'm not like my daughter. I feel fear."

"But Loki can't get to her anymore," George reasoned. "It's physically impossible."

"A few bars won't necessarily deter him," Tom

mumbled half to himself, his eyes darkening. "I know what my brother is capable of. We both know."

George took a sip of his own coffee. "But you're doing an excellent job protecting her."

Not really, Tom thought gloomily. The truth was, he should be watching her at all times. Even now. He realized he'd been fooling himself to think that Loki's minions were directionless. They could be anywhere and everywhere by now. Gaia wasn't aware of her uncle's powers. Nor the depth of his obsession.

"She thinks everything is fine now," Tom said sadly, looking into the dregs of his cup. "She's happy. She doesn't know the extent to which her uncle. . ." He didn't finish.

George leaned across the table. "We know where Loki is," he whispered. "We know what he's doing. We even know what he's eating for dinner tonight."

Tom shook his head. "But we also know something else about Loki." His knee was beginning to jiggle again, involuntarily. "We know that he's brilliant."

The Dinner Party

THE CLIP-ON TIE WAS PATENTLY absurd. But it was perfect nonetheless.

Loki surveyed the contents of his latest package,

delivered earlier this afternoon and concealed safely under his mattress. Until now. His various servants had excelled. Within seconds he shed his prison clothes and slipped into his freshly laundered, mattress-pressed, navy blue prison guard uniform. The tie was last: the proverbial icing on the cake.

He couldn't remember feeling this good in quite a while.

But there was no time to savor the moment. The schedule was too tight; every moment had to be perfectly choreographed. He tore open his packet of kerosene and then trickled the liquid over his bed, inhaling the odor as if it were the bouquet of a fine wine.

Now.

On cue, he began to hear the howls and screams of fellow prisoners.

Stepping quickly to his tiny window, he caught a quick glimpse of flame. A smile spread across his face. Flashes of bright orange light flickered through the windows of every cell. Black smoke began to stream through the cracks of the doors. `Everything was falling into place.` He grabbed his matchbook, lit one match, used it to light the rest of the matches—and then dropped the flaming matchbook onto the kerosene-covered bed.

Whoosh!

A burst of beautiful flame exploded atop the mattress in a blaze of yellow, orange, and indigo. Loki threw his dinner tray into the flames, followed by his old prison clothes. Thick black smoke billowed, slowly clouding up his cell. He coughed once, moving to the window again.

The piercing, shrill sounds of several alarms suddenly tore through the entire cell block. A herd of guards in black rubber gas masks stampeded into the hall. It was a scene of pure deafening, smoke-filled anarchy. Loki stood by the window and reveled in the chaos. The masked guards threw open the cell doors, each one spewing out mountains of thick smoke and crackling flames. There were scuffles as inmates bounced around the halls like uncaged animals. Billy clubs flew, smacking against raw flesh. Blood spilled. It was glorious. *Now, where is my guest?* Loki thought, coughing again. He tapped his foot impatiently.

As if in answer to his question, Loki's cell door came screeching open. A gas-masked guard stood before him.

"I've got this one!" the guard called, his voice muffled. He stepped quickly into Loki's cell.

"You're late," Loki snapped. "I could suffocate in here."

"I'm sorry, sir," the guard replied, bowing his head.

"Yes, well, let's get a look at you. Quickly, quickly!"

With a grunt the guard yanked off his gas mask.

Loki smiled once more, forgetting the smoke that

was burning his lungs. "Yes," he murmured, soaking in every detail of the man's face. *"Very good.* My compliments to the surgeon."

It wasn't exactly like looking in a mirror. But with the smoke and the panic and uncertainty. . . the bright blue eyes, the sturdy jaw. . . Loki could feasibly be looking at himself. Or Tom. For one brief moment Loki experienced a pang of unexpected rage. It took all his restraint not to bash the man's face in. In that instant Loki and Tom were face-to-face in the cell, and Loki was going to rip him limb from limb once and for all—put an end to his only legitimate obstacle—

"Come on," Loki ordered, sweeping the image from his mind. "Let's move. Strip and give me the mask."

The guest obliged: handing Loki the gas mask and ripping off his uniform, under which he was wearing inmate's clothes with Loki's prisoner number. He then threw his uniform into the flames. Loki buckled the gun holdster, then stretched the gas mask over his face.

"Thanks for your work," he murmured.

The double nodded.

Without warning, Loki lunged forward and seized the man's skull betweeen his hands, twisting it violently. There was a satisfying snap as the man's spine cracked, and his body went limp. Loki let him drop to

the floor. It was a pity to dispose of such a good oper-
ative, but there could be no loose ends. Loki darted
into the smoky hall—just as firefighters came running
through the flames, wielding fire extinguishers and
giant rubber hoses from the prison stairwells.

He grabbed one of the guards.

"One of the prisoners is unconscious!" he yelled
through his gas mask, with just the faintest hint of a
Brooklyn accent. "His cell is on fire! Better check on
him. I'm going for more backup!"

"Right!" the guard hollered back.

Adrenaline pumped through Loki's veins. He was
almost free. He made his way down the smoky
hall, running from the flames and prisoners and firefighters. . . until he reached a line of guards at the cell
block entrance.

"A ladder!" Loki hollered with a desperate urgency,
waving back at the fire. "Do you have a ladder?"

"Outside on the truck!" a firefighter replied.

"We need it *right now*," Loki barked. "I've got a
man trapped in there!"

"Right! Follow me!"

And with that, the fireman quite literally escorted
Loki, running, no less, through every single prison
checkpoint. He smiled behind the safety of his mask,
blinking as the streetlights hit him. Early evening. The
sky was a beautiful, dark blue. *The sky*.
Sky meant freedom. The road was inundated with

fire trucks, firefighters, police cars, and two ambulances. Loki's eyes flickered over both ambulances until he found what he was looking for: a black splotch of paint on the front bumper of the second one.

"The ladder's over here," the fireman yelled. "Can you. . ." He broke off as Loki collapsed to the pavement.

"What's wrong?" the firefighter demanded.

Loki convulsed, coughing, fogging up the plastic visor. "I. . . think some smoke. . . I don't know."

"I think you'd better stay out here!" the fireman hollered down at Loki. "Just tell me where the guy is."

"He's. . . *cough, cough, cough*. . . in. . . *cough*. . . cell block thirty-five. . . *cough*. . . upper level."

"Right! I'm on it." He glanced around the street and jerked a finger at Loki. "Someone take care of this man! I'm going back in!"

With that, an emergency medical technician—a young man of about twenty-five—hopped from the passenger side of the second ambulance.

"Come with me, okay?" he said. "I'm going to get you to the hospital."

Loki nodded, leaning against the young man as he staggered into the ambulance. He kept coughing, mostly for fear he would start laughing. The doors slammed shut, and then they were racing down the road, sirens raging.

The Manhattan federal jail disappeared in the distance.

174

"Are you all right, sir?" the young man asked.

"I'm fine," Loki replied, ripping the gas mask from his face and tearing the clip-on tie from his collar.

"Your clothes are in the drawer to the left, sir."

"Freshly laundered?"

"Of course, sir."

"Fine."

The ambulance bounced as it sped through the streets, but Loki managed to slip into a pair of black Armani pants and a sweater in less than a minute.

"Will you be needing anything else, sir?"

"Phone," Loki said.

"Right here, sir."

The young man handed back a minuscule black cell phone. Loki flipped it open and punched the memory dial.

"Yes?" a voice answered.

"Pick her up," he stated. "And take her to the safe house. Immediately." He closed the phone.

"Where to, sir, after we switch cars?" the driver asked.

"Back to the loft," Loki replied, gazing out the back window of the ambulance at the beautiful wide-open spaces. "But we'll make a stop at Tiffany's. I want to buy Gaia a gift. She's coming home."

His knuckles turned bone white as he gripped the armrests of his chair. The men **the** were running **truth** through to the children's playground, straight toward him.

AT LEAST HE SHOWED.

Almost Ashamed

Gaia felt a touch of her anger drain away as she watched the hunched, wheelchair-bound figure slowly rolling toward her across the shadowy playground. Just a touch. After all, she'd made it pretty clear in her note to Ed that if he didn't show, he'd get his ass kicked.

He slowed to a stop in front of her, his expression concealed by his bangs and by the darkness of early evening. He gazed at some invisible spot on the ground between them. "You wanted to talk. But I don't have much time. I—"

"Cut the bull, would you?"

Ed glanced up with his newly acquired classic sphinx stare. A stare that suggested everything but gave away nothing.

Gaia sighed. "I have a question for you, Ed. It might sound familiar. The question is this: Where is Ed Fargo, and what have you done with him?"

A flicker of something like humor crossed Ed's face but was instantly replaced with pain. Then he shook his head, slipping once more into a mask of nothingness. "I'm just under a lot of stress," he said. The words were empty, hackneyed, without meaning. "I'm—"

"Bullshit," Gaia spat. "You're just under a lot of bullshit right now. That's why you can't talk, right? Give it up, Ed!"

178

Her voice rose, ricocheting angrily off the metal jungle gyms and swings. "Either you talk or I'm out of here—"

"Gaia!"

Gaia wheeled around to see Sam. And for the first time in what seemed like days, he was actually smiling. Instantly her face lit up. She hadn't expected to see him before dinner. Of course, now wasn't a good time....

Uh-oh. She frowned. Something was wrong. As he drew closer, she could see that his smile was strained. Contrite. Almost ashamed.

"Gaia." He stood before her, his eyes everywhere but on her—on Ed, on the chess tables, on the moon rising in the purple sky. "I can't come tonight. To dinner."

Can't. Come.

The words fell heavy on her ears. But surprisingly, she felt absolutely nothing. Only as if her whole body had suddenly hollowed out and inverted, left empty.

"I'm sorry," Sam added. "This is beyond my control. I can't get out of—"

"Save it," Gaia shot back. Her mind twisted around Sam's words. *Can't.* People always used *can't* when in fact they meant *won't.* A few seconds passed. Sam opened his mouth again, but Gaia cut him off him by turning her back. Enough. No more pain. She had her quirks, but masochism wasn't one of them. Besides, any speech from Sam would be pointless because with Sam, words carried no weight. He'd just take them back later.

Sam's hand went to her shoulder. She didn't try to knock it off, but she didn't react, either. She simply stared at Ed—who looked very much like he wished he were somewhere else. She could relate.

And then Sam was gone.

Gaia refused to flinch at the sound of Sam's dying footsteps. It was better to act like nothing had happened. Better to act like Sam hadn't broken yet another promise. That he hadn't let her down tonight of all nights. Yes. . . it was better to replace one disappointment with another—one she could no longer avoid: Ed. He sat still and silent as a mummy.

Gaia sighed.

"This mystery-man thing is wearing thin," she said in a dry, flinty voice she barely recognized as her own. "Now, are you also going to continue to be an asshole, or is someone around here going to cut me a break and start talking instead of lying?"

THE TRUTH SHALL SET YOU FREE.

The truth shall also make your life way more complicated than it is already, and you shall suffer as a result.

Out-of-Body

But lying was hardly an easy way out. And it definitely wasn't pain-free.

Ed clenched his jaw as Gaia glared at him. She was way beyond pissed. And she had a right to be. And Ed would basically do everything short of selling his soul to Satan to tell her. To come clean about everything.

Of course, in a way he had sold his soul. For $26 million.

"Well?" Gaia prompted. "Do you have anything to say, or am I just wasting my time?"

I think I can walk, Gaia. I've been cutting class to work on my rehab. I've been lying because Heather is making me. She wants my money—

"I've been keeping secrets from you," Ed began slowly. "But for a good reason."

Gaia arched an eyebrow and waited. Even angry, even in the terrible light of the Washington Square park lamps, Gaia looked beautiful—her skin like ivory, her body so strong and sexy. Ed felt the thud of his own conflicted heart, pounding relentlessly. In three seconds he could change that hostile look of hers into total delight. He could transform Gaia from adversary back into best friend. And in those same three seconds he could betray Heather. Not to mention the small fact of unhatched chickens. What if he *couldn't* walk? What if verbalizing his tenuous hopes jinxed the whole thing?

"I'm listening." Gaia folded her arms.

"I've been holding out on you because I'm afraid if I tell you what's happening, you'll judge somebody too harshly," Ed whispered, forcing himself to meet her gaze. "And the person you might judge is someone I've sworn to protect."

Gaia stared back at him. Her face softened. "Don't you trust me?"

Ed nodded.

"What if I promise to keep both my judgment and your secret to myself?" Gaia offered. "Could you tell me then?"

"I. . ." Ed swallowed. She would keep his secret; he wasn't worried about that. But Ed didn't have as much faith in her inability to suspend judgment. Especially when it came to Heather Gannis. But maybe it was time to stop protecting other people and start worrying about himself. If it meant giving up on his friendship with Gaia, then maybe the price on Heather's love was just too high. Twenty-six million dollars he could sacrifice. But not Gaia.

"G, I really want to tell you what's happening," Ed choked out. He leaned forward in his chair, his eyes sparkling at the thought of sharing his news with the one person who could truly share in his joy. But instantly that thought was replaced by Heather's face—and Ed found himself totally deflated. He paused, wiped a hand across his dry mouth. "I want to tell. So badly. You don't understand what this has been doing to me—"

The shrill screech of brakes pierced the air. A black van had pulled up next to the curb. Ed scowled at it. Just his luck. One of the most crucial moments of his life had been interrupted by that particular breed of insane drivers that seemed to exist only in New York.

A sliding door opened.

Two men in black ski masks jumped out.

What the. . . ? Ed's stomach lurched. His knuckles turned bone white as he gripped the armrests of his chair. The men were running through to the children's playground, straight toward him. But they were staring at Gaia.

His head snapped up at her.

"Sit tight," Gaia muttered, shooting Ed a quick half smile at her weak joke.

Ed's throat closed. He thought about trying to roll away, but he couldn't move. And he wouldn't abandon Gaia. Never. The men closed in on them. He was in shock. Should he shout for help? There was no one nearby. Too cold and wet for kids and mothers in the playground. *Lucky for them,* Ed thought grimly.

"You're coming with us," the man on the left spat at Gaia.

They approached her from either side.

"Play nice and you won't get hurt," the second thug added, flapping his coat to reveal a gun nestled in the waistband of his pants.

"Yeah, okay," Gaia mumbled. She bowed her head.

Ed gaped at her. His shock overcame his fear. Gaia going gently? Where was the kung fu, the karate, the ass kicking? Ever since Ed had known Gaia, bad guys with guns had trailed after her like a pack of dogs. And most of the time she'd left them lying on the street in bloody heaps. Maybe this was a trick. Ed chewed his dry lip. Yeah, it must be—

"Just let me walk on my own, okay?" Gaia muttered. The two men took her arms, one each side. "Move," they ordered simultaneously.

Okay. Ed's pulse raced. Okay. . . maybe this wasn't a trick. Maybe Gaia was really surrendering. Maybe she'd disappear into that black van and he'd never see her again. Terrified, he strained forward in his chair. He had to do something, but what? Gaia's blond hair fell in a curtain, blocking her face from view. She took a few steps toward the van. Then abruptly she stopped and lashed out with a kick, tripping up the thug on her right.

"Yes!" Ed screamed, elated.

As the guy fumbled for his gun and fought to regain his balance, Gaia shook free of the other one, simultaneously burying her elbow in his solar plexus. He grunted and doubled over. *Damn!* Ed blinked at the speed of Gaia's movements. Whirling, she delivered a roundhouse kick to the first guy, planting her foot into his skull with an audible crack. He fell forward, his chin eating tar, the gun skating across the gravel walkway and knocking against a bench. He was out cold. But the other guy had already recovered.

"Behind you!" Ed shouted.

The man's arm swooped through the air in a punch. But Gaia was faster. She blocked the move with her left arm at his wrist. She grasped firmly with her right hand, pulled, and, using the guy's own momentum, flipped him over her head. Ed found himself smiling as the guy's body thumped to the hard ground. More amazing even than the force of her moves was Gaia's grace and speed. But it wasn't over. The man raised his head—and managed to grasp her foot as she delivered a follow-up kick. With a twist he tackled her. Suddenly they were rolling away from Ed, a tumble of legs and arms, with Gaia trying to counter her opponent's weight with her own strength—

Oh, shit.

Out of the corner of his eye Ed spotted movement. The other guy had stirred and was inching on his stomach across the ground toward. . . no. God, no. Dread seized Ed's insides in a cold grip. This was horribly wrong. He opened his mouth to call out, but his voice had been robbed of speech. Gaia was pinned down; he couldn't even see her face. And the second thug was steadily crawling toward the gun, glinting there in the lamplight.

Ed's eyes closed the gap between the gun and himself.

Not far away. Maybe ten feet. *Far enough.* He wouldn't make it. Not if he dragged his body by the strength of his arms. Not unless he walked. But Ed hadn't moved more than four steps without support.

He couldn't do it now.

Now. It had to be now. The crawling man still had some ground to cover. Ed couldn't hesitate. He had to make a move. A move he knew his body couldn't manage.

Gaia slammed her head into her opponent's and rolled out and away from him. He lay there beside her, lifeless. Only. . . she was lifeless, too. Not moving. Hardly even *breathing.* Ed's own breath came in rapid-fire gasps. He closed his eyes, willing every ounce of energy he had into his numb legs. He needed more than an adrenaline rush. He had that already. He needed a miracle.

Gaia.

He pushed himself from the chair. Pain seared his legs—a fiery, intense agony, far worse than any of his sessions with Brian. The air around him seemed to go black. The park spun, blurred in a kaleidoscope of shiny tar and wet leaves and a voice saying something about the cripple. . . . *Am I walking?* It felt more out-of-body than a real, physical experience. *The pain. The pain.* It was all-consuming. He wasn't walking. He was just wishing himself there, his hands snatching at the air, at. . . silver. Ed's hands closed on the gun as he hit the gravel, crumpling, the cold metal in his clammy fingers a sudden, beautiful hard-edged clarity.

The pain began to recede.

Using his last bit of strength Ed spun his upper body into a sitting position. The world refocused. His hands shook, but he had the gun. He pointed it straight at the crawling man's head. There was no sound. Just wind and Ed's own deep breathing. No movement. The crawling man froze, the whites of his eyes registering fear.

Is this real?

Ed swallowed, jostling for some concrete proof of what seemed like one long surrealistic movie montage. Then he became aware of movement again. . . Gaia had stumbled to her feet, a smear of blood across her cheek, her startled blue eyes staring.

He glanced up at her for a split second, then turned his eyes back to the man on the ground.

"You. . . Ed, you can. . ." Gaia shook her head. She started weaving. Her eyes lolled. And as if in slow motion, she crumpled from the waist. Her knees caved, and she struck the ground. But she emitted one final gasping word before falling unconscious.

". . . walk?"

"Yes," Ed murmured.

The secret was out. But so was Gaia.

And with a little luck, she wouldn't remember a thing.

TOM DETECTED THE SOFT PURR OF

the approaching car even before he caught a glimpse of it—a black BMW—reflected in the rear window of a parked van. The headlights

An Act of Noncompliance

were off. Instantly Tom's senses were on high alert, scoping Mercer Street for any available cover. There was none. The dimly lit sidewalk was deserted. Perfect for an assassination. He reached for the nine-millimeter pistol tucked into his inside coat pocket. It was too late to make a break for his apartment building; the entrance was still a good thirty paces from his current position. The BMW would be alongside him in seconds. His eyes darted to the van. He could hide behind it until a pedestrian—

"Enigma!"

George. Tom froze in his tracks. Instinctively he knew this was a stupid move: George's voice could easily be duplicated, and Tom's enemies were all well aware of his code name. Besides, George almost never referred to Tom as "Enigma," not even when they were working. But there was a note of undeniable urgency in that voice—one that would be difficult to fake. Tom whirled to see George's head emerging from the passenger-side window.

"Get in," George hissed as the car screeched to a halt behind the van.

Tom swallowed. After only the briefest hesitation he jumped into the backseat of the BMW and slammed the door behind him. The car lurched back into traffic. Tom's eyes flashed to the driver in the rearview mirror; she was an Agency woman in her midthirties, but he couldn't place her name. He had only met her briefly on a few occasions. He remembered that she was an expert in languages.

"What's going on?" Tom demanded, fighting to keep his voice steady.

"We're taking you to JFK," George answered.

"Why? What on earth—"

"Loki's been sprung," George interrupted.

Tom stopped breathing. He found he couldn't speak. He wasn't shocked, of course; in a way, he'd expected as much. No, he was simply terrified—and not for himself. *Gaia.* She was home; at least, that's where he assumed she was, getting ready for their big dinner tonight. And *he* was stuck in this car. Away from her. Unable to protect her. And Loki—

"He escaped about forty-five minutes ago," George continued. "There was a fire in the jail. He had a double on the inside. They just found the body—"

"Take me to my apartment," Tom commanded.

George peered around the back of his seat. Fear was etched into every line of his worn face. "We can't, Tom. We have to get you on a plane to London."

Tom shook his head. His jaw tightened. "I'm not leaving without Gaia," he stated. "So take me to my apartment. *Now.*"

"I'm sorry," George whispered. He exchanged a quick glance with the driver. "I'm afraid we don't have a choice here."

Hot rage coiled inside Tom's chest. "Either you take me to my apartment or I'm jumping out of this car," he whispered between tightly clenched teeth.

The driver's eyes met Tom's in the rearview mirror.

"I have orders to terminate you, sir, if you do not comply," she stated.

Tom blinked. She'd sounded very matter-of-fact— as any good agent would. And in that instant he had no doubt that she would carry out her orders. She and Tom had no personal history; she felt no loyalty to him. That was probably why the Agency had assigned her to this mission, because killing him would be no problem for her. This was business. Nothing more. Tom should have expected it: His relationship with his superiors had become strained at best. In spite of a lifetime of service. In spite of every sacrifice imaginable. But this was not the time for bitterness or resentment. He drew in a deep breath.

"What's going on?" he asked again.

"A situation has developed in Europe," the driver

answered. "We've traced a series of payments from one of Loki's phony corporations to a team of German scientists, three of whom were found murdered this morning. They worked for NATO and the German defense ministry. That's all I can tell you."

Tom shot a hard glare at George. "How long have you known this?"

George shook his head. "I found out ten minutes ago," he mumbled.

For a moment Tom just stared at his old friend. Then he leaned back in his seat. His options swirled before him like dead leaves on a breezy autumn day—quickly crumbling in the wind. He could try to escape now and be killed. He could try to escape at the airport or on assignment, in which case he'd be hunted down and killed as well. If he didn't obey orders, he would wind up dead. No. . . his only choice was to stay alive, to complete this mission. Only then could he possibly see Gaia again.

Tom's chest tightened. His eyes began to smart. The Agency knew very well what they were doing. They were blackmailing him with his daughter's life. The mission was inextricably bound up with Gaia's safety—because if Loki was free to oversee whatever foul scheme he was planning in Europe, then he was free to snatch Gaia as well.

"At the very least. . . at the very least, let—let me say good-bye," Tom stammered. His voice caught in his throat. "Please, George. Do me this one favor. The Agency owes—"

"Two minutes," the woman interrupted. She jerked the steering wheel hard to the right, and the car skidded onto Canal Street. "I'll give you two minutes with your daughter. Any more than that and I'll have to consider this an act of noncompliance. Understood?"

Tom nodded. But he couldn't answer. He was crying.

Never mind the
fact that two
psychos had
tried to kidnap
her. Never **alien**
mind that she
didn't have **surge**
a clue as to
who they were
or what they
wanted.

GAIA FELT LIKE SHE WAS STILL

unconscious. Yes, she'd been
awake for several minutes
now, and her attackers were
long gone. . . but *this,* this
was just too outrageous to be
true. It had to be a dream.
Not just Ed's walking. All of

Dark Possibility

it—everything that had tumbled from Ed's mouth as
he sat there beside her, still clutching the gun: the
secret, the reason he'd kept it to himself, his bargain
with Heather—

"Gaia? Did you hear what I just said?"

She shook her head, unable to stop staring at him.
"Huh?"

"Who *were* those guys?" he demanded.

"I. . ." She shrugged. She had no idea. Besides, the
question struck her as extremely unimportant, given
the circumstances. "I just can't believe Heather asked
you to do that, Ed. It's just. . . it's just beyond my com-
prehension—"

"Gaia!" Ed barked. "They had guns. They almost
killed you. They could have killed me. What the hell is
going on?"

She stared at him, but all she could do was shrug
again. It pained her. She could see the genuine fear in
his eyes. He deserved an answer to the question. So
did she. Her mind kept coming back to Loki, of

course. . . but he was in jail. So were there sickos in the world who wanted a piece of Gaia Moore? This was a dark possibility she'd really never considered. But it seemed pretty clear: She had an enemy who wanted her kidnapped.

"Ed," Gaia said softly, dropping all her attitude for a brief moment for Ed's sake. "I don't know who they were, and I don't know what they wanted, okay? Hopefully I will find those answers—either by myself or with my father's help. But right now the important thing is that I'm okay and you're okay. And. . . and you saved my life."

Those last words were difficult. She had to wrestle them from deep inside her. And she knew the reason: She never found it easy to admit that she couldn't handle every situation with complete autonomy. But now, with all her new and completely screwed-up attachments, life was much more complicated.

"Thanks," she whispered.

"Yeah, well, now we're even," Ed muttered. Then he smiled and gingerly placed the gun on the ground beside them, pointing in the opposite direction. "Besides, that's some of the best walking I've done in years."

Gaia could only shake her head—once again reliving that image of Ed on his feet. Playing it in her mind, rewinding it, and playing it again. It was all unbelievable. The fact that Ed could walk. The fact that he'd saved her life. Or the fact that Heather Gannis was trying to take Ed's accident settlement. Especially the part about Heather. . .

Correction. Heather's being a selfish schemer? Not so unbelievable. *Ed can walk.* That was truly the wildest part of this equation. Gaia had thought she was hallucinating in the park, watching Ed pick himself up out of his wheelchair and shuffle forward. She'd thought for sure she'd damaged her skull in the fight somehow and was experiencing some kind of neurological breakdown. Her eyes wandered over to the wheelchair, sitting there in the darkness like a discarded toy.

"You're amazing," she heard herself say.

Ed smiled again, and for a brief, shining moment everything in the world was okay. Never mind Sam. Never mind the fact that two psychos had tried to kidnap her. Never mind that she didn't have a clue as to who they were or what they wanted. She had her best friend back, Ed could walk, and right now she felt happy and so damn proud of Ed that she wanted to stand up and tell the whole city what he'd just pulled off. *Listen up, New York: My friend Ed is a walking miracle!*

"Hey," Ed warned. There was an edge in his tone. "You promised you wouldn't tell anyone my secret. And you also promised not to judge Heather."

She sighed, not sure if she wanted to laugh or to

punch him. "Are you seriously telling me you're going to go through with this hush-hush garbage? Come on. You can't do this to yourself. If you're going to walk again—"

"And this is not your decision to make," Ed interrupted. "I'm not asking for your approval, G. But I am asking you to keep your promises. You swore you'd keep my secret. You swore you wouldn't judge."

She opened her mouth, then closed it. *Mental note: Stop making promises you know you'll regret.* "You know I won't breathe squat to anyone. But as for not judging Heather. . ." She frowned. "No can do."

"Just keep it to yourself," he mumbled.

Right. Easier said than done. It would take every ounce of self-control that Gaia possessed not to have a little talk with Heather. But a promise was a promise. To break it would be to become like Sam Moon. And that was not a move she was prepared to make.

"You play hardball," Gaia finally said with a grim smile. "I might have to kick you."

Ed laughed. "I might have to kick you back."

AS SOON AS THE FEDEX GUY WAS

Acrid Taste

out of sight, Sam hauled the massive box from the hall into the living room of B4, then ran into his room to get a penknife. Delivery from the police station. He knew exactly what it was. His computer. Back at last. He crouched beside the box and ran the blade along the cardboard lid, feeling a swell of relief.

After a day of complete and utter shit, it felt good to have some minor redemptive moment. The police had returned his computer, which meant he was now officially and completely in the clear as far as Mike's death was concerned.

With a groan Sam lugged the monitor over to his desk and started rewiring the machine. No doubt the assholes had completely wiped his hard drive. No doubt they'd read every personal piece of e-mail he'd ever written. Whatever. Those were small prices to pay, comparatively. He'd learned to live with minor disappointments.

The big ones, he still had trouble with.

Sam swallowed hard, an acrid taste in the back of his mouth. Again he tried to wipe out the image of Gaia's face from his mind—her expression of disgust as she'd turned away from him in the park. But he couldn't. It had been playing on an endless loop. How the hell was he going to mend their relationship? Maybe he couldn't. Maybe it really was over. If Gaia had treated Sam the way he'd been treating her for the past week. . .

Well, he'd still forgive her. He loved her too much.

Which made it all the more painful. Because he could completely understand it if she never forgave *him.* He started grinding his teeth as he hooked up the various cables, the image of Gaia's face melting in his mind, shifting into an image of Josh Kendall. Every ounce of Sam's pain was thanks to that bastard and the people who paid him. If their plan was to destroy Sam's life, they had succeeded. Why couldn't they leave him alone?

Almost without thinking, Sam grabbed the phone and punched in Gaia's number. This was call number five in less than an hour. Again the machine picked up. He slammed the phone back down on the hook. She was probably blowing off steam somewhere or telling Ed what a big-time loser Sam was.

He looked at his watch. 7:00 P.M.

Enough of this shit. He wasn't going to spend Friday night hooking up his computer or loitering in his suite just because Josh had ordered him to do so. No, something inside him had just snapped. If this were a chess game, he could surely find his way out of a check. He'd played plenty of games where opponents thought they'd had him mated. They'd be sure the game was over, and then Sam would find a move they hadn't seen. One brilliant move.

Of course, this wasn't a game.

That was the entire point. This was real life. Maybe in chess Sam needed a brilliant move, but in life all he needed. . . was Gaia. So in a way there was a simple and uncomplicated solution: *Find her.*

Right. Sam grabbed the white shirt draped across the ironing board in his room. As he buttoned it, he felt an alien surge of a feeling long forgotten: hope. Coupled with some kind of manic courage. Or maybe it was straight lunacy. Was there even a difference? Not really. Leaving could very well mean suicide. But at this point he was starting to wonder if death was preferable to this. . . this *nonlife* he was living.

Josh would be calling any minute—turning up with instructions, threats on Gaia's life, and whatever other surprises he had in store. But Sam would be long gone. If he didn't find Gaia at her place, then he'd find her at the restaurant.

And confess.

I wonder how Ed will change now that he can walk.

Maybe he'll be the same. Maybe he'll turn back into the skater formerly known as Shred, the badass who drove the girls of the Lower East Side crazy, who won the heart of Heather Gannis. Or maybe he'll be somebody completely different.

All I can say for certain is that he won't be the wiseass in the wheelchair that I've come to know and love. And that's disconcerting.

Scratch that. That's unbelievably selfish. This is the greatest breakthrough possible, and here I am wondering how it will affect *me*. Ed doesn't need more selfishness. Clearly he's getting it on all sides from Heather. No surprise there, although Ed wasn't expecting it. With one tug on his heartstrings, she retains the cash flow to which she thinks she is entitled. Actually that's not so

surprising, either. Ed is stu-
pidly generous and a total
sucker for sentiment. Heather
takes advantage; Ed knows it,
yet he just goes along with her,
anyway. Because that's Ed.
Always putting everyone else
first.

I think Ed is the only
unselfish person that I know.
Except for my dad.

Heather, Sam, and me—we're all
narcissists.

A thousand
horrible
scenarios
whirled
through his **the**
head at
once, **positives**
all
revolving
around. . .
them.

"DAD?" GAIA CALLED.

This is going to suck. Gaia pushed open the front door of the Mercer apartment and pocketed her key. She'd been dreading this moment: the inevitable confession. Now she'd have to tell her dad how Sam had stood them up for dinner. And then there would be some kind of sympathy moment during which her father would spot the cut on her head. And then there would be a stream of questions that she (*a*) couldn't answer and (*b*) didn't feel like facing.

One Day

Bath. Hot bubble bath. Three hours long. That was all she wanted.

Which, judging from the darkness, she would be able to get after all.

Yes. Gaia ripped off her coat and hit the bathroom, eager to fill the tub before her father got in. That way they could talk more distantly through the bathroom door and maybe avoid some of the mandatory fatherly concern factor. It wasn't that Gaia didn't like the idea of fatherly concern. She just needed to be alone. Anyway, what could her father say that she didn't already know? Sam had let her down. Broken his word. And her heart. Case closed.

She sighed, a slow ache burning up through her heart as she stared at the running water. She thought of all the clichés people said at moments like these, clichés that only made the pain worse. *If it looks too good to be true, then it is too good to be true.* Gaia almost laughed at that one. Sam had always looked too good.

It was over, though. She needed to accept it and move on. Like she had so many times before, with so many other losses. She forced herself out of the bathroom at a brisk walk, steering her thoughts away from him. Tonight she would have a nice dinner with her father. Tonight she would savor the good things. The positives. Speaking of which, it *was* kind of weird that her father wasn't back yet.

Gaia switched on the living-room light. Her eye fell on a piece of white paper, propped up on the mantel above the fireplace. She smiled. Ever since her dad had reentered her life, he'd become extra cautious about informing her of his every move. If he was late at all— even by a minute, even for the most trivial reason—he overapologized for it.

Poor Dad. Gaia's smile twisted sadly. He was still trying to make up for the way he'd disappeared from her life without a trace. She knew he wasn't over his guilt yet. Five years was a long time. But one day. . .

Gaia lifted the note.

My dearest Gaia,
    By the time you read this, I will be gone. I cannot tell you where I am going or when I will

be back—only that I am going to London first. From there I will try to call before I am transferred somewhere else. They will not tell me where for fear that I will tell you. Please believe me when I say that I have no loyalty to anyone or anything but you—that my life as I once lived it is over. I suppose that in a way, it ended the moment we lost your mother. But that is a conversation for another time, another place.

I do everything for you, for your protection. If I am to see you ever again, I must go now.

I don't expect you to understand. If it were in my power to take you and run and be free of this life, I would. All that matters to me is your safety. But in order to ensure it, I must remain alive. George will take care of you for now. I trust him. I will return as soon as humanly possible.

My darling, forgive me, especially for leaving tonight of all nights. Know that I am thinking of you, that I remain always,

Your loving
Dad

With shaking hands, Gaia dropped the piece of paper to the floor.

Incredibly, though, she felt no pain. No sadness. Just resignation. She should have seen this coming.

She had been naive, deluded, and just plain illogical, staking her hopes of permanence on a man who disappeared for a living. And as always, her father had chosen the world over her. His love was an illusion. It looked pretty, handwritten there on his note—but it was just a word, void of feeling. Gaia flicked the light switch, plunging the room into darkness. It warmed her, enveloped her, shutting out everyone and everything else. She stood silent and still in the empty living room.

But then she noticed her cheeks were wet.

She was crying. Salty tears streamed down her face. But she still felt nothing. It was simply a physical reaction, a reflex. Maybe she could no longer feel sadness, either. Maybe sadness had gone the way of fear. That would be a relief. Then she wouldn't have any more trouble. Then she really *would* be the "new" Gaia she so desperately wanted to be. Accept it and move on. Accept it and move on. The words were her own private mantra, as soothing as a poem—

Knock, knock.

Someone was here.

Get lost, she silently told the unwelcome visitor. But the knocking was persistent. George. Or maybe the kidnappers from earlier. Who knew, and who cared? Gaia sprang to her feet and threw open the front door, hoping it was a bunch of Jehovah's Witnesses ready to take her away to a better life. . . or a serial killer waiting to put her out of her misery. Bring it on. Because anything was better than this, and nothing could be worse.

But at that moment she realized she was wrong.

Because that was when it broke: "it" being the last feeble string that held her together.

SAM BARELY OPENED HIS MOUTH before Gaia collapsed into his arms, sobbing. Terror consumed him instantly. He'd never seen Gaia so distraught—never seen anything close to this display of emotion.

The Limit

A thousand horrible scenarios whirled through his head at once, all revolving around... *them.*

"What is it?" Sam begged, practically carrying Gaia's limp body toward the couch. "Gaia? Did someone try to hurt you?"

"He's gone," she wept. "He's gone—"

"Who?" Sam demanded, holding her tightly to him, smoothing down her hair, doing anything he could to soothe her as her tears flowed down his shirt. He sat her down on the couch. "Who's gone, Gaia? You have to tell me."

"My father. He's gone, Sam. . . . He's gone again."

"It's okay," Sam whispered, tightening his arms around her as she curled up inside his embrace. He swallowed. He was here now. Here to hold her for as long as she needed. "It's okay. I've got you, Gaia. I'm—"

"No," Gaia choked out, shoving Sam away and scrambling to her feet.

Sam gaped at her, uncomprehending. "What?" he whispered.

"That's the problem, Sam. You're here now."

"What. . . what are you talking about?" he asked.

"You're here, and then you're gone. Just like him. Just like my father."

Sam shook his head rapidly. "It's not at all what you think, Gaia. I can explain. That's all over now. That's why I'm here, to explain it all to—"

"Explain *what?*" Gaia interrupted. She savagely wiped her tears from her face and sniffed. "Explain that you haven't been yourself, that you've been avoiding me? Give me some lame excuse about some secret crisis you're going through? It's all bullshit, Sam!" Her voice rose to a shriek. "All of it!"

The words slapped him with an almost palpable force. He leaned back in the cushions, lips quivering. He blinked, searching for a response, a remedy, *anything*. But he couldn't deny what she'd said. Could he? He refused to let himself believe that their relationship had been damaged beyond the point of no return.

They were just getting started. They had an entire future together—a series of tender moments and intimacy and sharing, all laid before him in perfection, like the squares on a chessboard. He wouldn't let that slip away. It was more than a vision; it was reality. In the end, love could overcome deception. Especially when the deception was justified...

"I love you," he heard himself say. It was all he had left.

But Gaia just laughed grimly. "Well. Look what all this love has done to me. It's made me *weak*. And I am not weak, Sam. I am not weak."

Sam bit his lip, staring up at Gaia's wet face. She was without question the strongest girl he'd ever known—the strongest girl he ever *would* know. And in that one brief moment of silence he fell twice as much in love with her. As if moving in a dream, he stood up from the couch and stepped toward her. "Do you have any idea how much—"

"It *doesn't matter*," Gaia spat. She moved away from him, inching in the direction of the door. "Not in the end. We have to start over. Alone. Apart. It's the only way."

"Gaia—"

"No," she stated, backing away until she was in the doorway. "You can pick any kind of story you want for me, for us, whatever. But my story always ends the same way, Sam. With me alone. That's the way it has to be. That's the only way I'll survive."

"I won't let you," he insisted, springing forward and grabbing her wrist. "You have to—"

"Let me *go!*" she howled, turning and striking his arm with her free hand. Her fingers struck a pressure point: A tingle shot down the entire length of his bone, and his arm seemed to go limp and numb. Sam's jaw dropped.

In that split second she flung open the door and ran.

Sam stood there, watching her disappear down the hall, clutching the spot where she'd struck him. His heart pounded; his head swam. He was left standing in the middle of this apartment. He knew he had to move, to chase her.

But he couldn't.

And there was one simple reason. The saddest possible reason.

She didn't want him to chase her. She didn't want him at all. Her actions had spoken for her.

The Zen Approach

"IS THIS SOME KIND OF JOKE?"

Loki hissed into the speaker phone as he paced the length of a Chelsea loft. The voice on the other end jabbered weak apology after weak apology,

211

but Loki was barely listening. What incompetency! A *cripple* overpowering his men for hire? *My God.* The botched kidnapping was so remarkable as to be almost comical. Indeed, if the stakes weren't so high, Loki might simply have thrown back his head and had a good laugh at the image of Gaia's little paraplegic pal scampering out of his wheelchair and subduing two professional thugs. The kid had courage; Loki had to give him that.

And a pair of working legs as well, it seemed.

"You let her get away," Loki snapped. He fired each word as if they were bullets, letting the full implication of the sentence sink in. Capturing Gaia should have been the least of his troubles. Far more challenging was the prison escape. Far more challenging was the very idea of winning Gaia back emotionally.

"Please," the tinny voice on the other end pleaded. "You don't—"

"What am I paying you for?" Loki roared. He slammed his fist down on the top of a stainless steel desk. His blazing eyes swept the large, industrial space—with its twenty-foot-high ceilings and spare furnishings.

Everything was in order. Everything was just as he needed it to be. A leather-and-aluminum Mies van der Rohe couch. A glass coffee table. A fully stocked kitchen. Gaia's little room all ready for her, complete with fresh tulips in a Caledon vase. Loki had stipulated his needs and been pleased to see how thoroughly his wishes had been granted, right down to the details of his particular aesthetic vis-à-vis home furnishings.

But without Gaia, there was no reason for any of it.

He picked up a glass ashtray and hurled it at the exposed-brick wall. It shattered with a violent crash, sending shards of glass flying.

"We know where she is," the voice on the other end of the telephone broke in hurriedly. "She has been spotted crying on a bench in the park. She is there as we speak. Totally alone. And we can—"

"Alone?"

Loki straightened and turned with interest back to the speaker phone, breathing hard to dispel some part of his rage. He needed to think clearly. Gaia was supposed to be dining with Tom. Yet she was in the park. Curious.

"Crying?" he asked.

"Yes, sir. She seems very upset about something. We have our men ready to retrieve her on command."

Loki thought for a moment. Then he smiled. "No. That will be all."

"I'm sorry? You said—"

Loki disconnected the call, poured himself a glass of Riesling, and walked over to the windows. Perhaps the botched kidnapping had served a purpose after all.

The Zen approach.

Yes. . . if Gaia was crying alone in the park instead

of having cozy dinners with her father and boyfriend, then it seemed the world had disappointed her again. And indeed if that were the case, then there would be no need to continue with the kidnapping. Being captured would only alienate Gaia from Loki further. No. He had to play this situation to his advantage. She would come of her own accord. When she was ready. He sipped his wine thoughtfully, gazing out at the skyline twinkling from across the Hudson. New Jersey. Not the most splendid skyline in the world, but it would do for now.

We shall go with the flow.

Loki's smile widened as he thought of a moment in the not-too-distant future when he and Gaia would share a fine wine together. When she would let him comfort her. Soothe her fears and ease all of her doubts. Murmur sympathies for all the cruelty that had come her way. Reassure her that neither Tom nor Sam Moon would be able to hurt her anymore.

And happy and safe at last, Gaia would be ready for the next step. Ready to be shaped for her destiny.

Beloved Gaia. Loki toasted her silently, raising his glass in the darkness. *I have big plans for you.*

It's amazing how stupid you can be when you want something bad enough. Take me, thinking I could have happiness for longer than a minute. Who was I kidding?

Myself. I was kidding myself. Because when all of this happiness stuff began, I truly believed I could hold on to it. Long term. But anything long term is just not built into my life plan.

After all that's happened, a couple of truths have become abundantly clear: Trusting in love is a liability I can no longer afford. Not now, not ever. Trust, period, is becoming a liability. The only people who never let me down—my mother and Mary—are both dead. Maybe that's *why* they never let me down. Maybe they just didn't have the chance.

Morbid thought, but hey, might as well be honest.

Camus said it, and I'm inclined to agree. Life really is a solitary mission—an absurd,

random search without meaning—one
that each person ultimately
undertakes alone. Looking at it
any other way is just buying into
an illusion meant to make you
feel safe when you're not. Like
religion. Or love.

So I'm changing my goals and
philosophies to reflect my actual
life, not my fantasy life. I
won't have to be careful what I
wish for anymore. Because the
time for wishing is over.

I remember the day Gaia first learned to walk. When her little legs took their first wobbly steps, Katia and I were thrilled, like any parents would be. But we were also concerned. Gaia was only seven months old.

That was only the beginning, of course. The first clue.

As Gaia's mental and physical abilities grew in leaps and bounds, I became conflicted. Though I encouraged my daughter, I was also afraid for her because she was clearly exceptional. And exceptional people court danger. They cannot live a truly free life. I know this firsthand. Exceptional people can use their powers to help others. Or else they are themselves a danger to others, like Loki.

Loki.

I was right not to underestimate him. Even when George tried to placate me, I knew the story wasn't over. I knew that Oliver was far from safely incarcerated.

And now my brother and I are headed for a battle of wills that has barely even begun. Worst of all, far worse than any fear or pain is that I know Gaia must hate me right now.

How could she not? She has her emotions to contend with, memories of my abandonment of her. And she also doesn't understand the challenges that lie ahead for me, challenges I cannot avoid because of who I am. If she knew the facts, perhaps she would hate me less. I like to think so. But she cannot know.

All I can do is send her silent messages, willing her to think the best of me because I love her. That love is the force that guides me always, for better or for worse. Sitting on this plane, I keep scrolling through all the choices I've made in my life—every one of them leading me to this moment. I wonder if I could have made any of them differently in order to be the sort of father my daughter craves.

But in my heart of hearts I know I am powerless to change what was already written into the story long before my daughter was even born.

Gaia, I know you just wanted a normal life, as did I, but we are not normal people, and apparently it was not to be. And I beg of you, whatever you think, please find a way to believe in me. I'm going to need your faith for the road ahead. Because if I've learned anything in my life, it's that the best man doesn't always win; good doesn't always triumph over evil. Life isn't fair.

here is a
sneak peek of
Fearless™ #16:
NAKED

A funny thing happened to me the other day. (Was it yesterday?) I woke up, showered, scarfed down two bowls of Froot Loops, and went to school. For some reason, though, the doors were locked and the building was empty.

And then I remembered. It was Saturday.

Ha ha ha. Hysterical, right?

Guess you had to be there.

I can't seem to keep track of time anymore. For example, I know my father left a few days ago. I'm just not sure how many days it was. Four? Five? Six? Not that it matters. He'll probably be gone for another five years, or ten, or forever. And I suspect that if I had some adult supervision—if I weren't just living in solitude in a big, two-bedroom sublet on Mercer Street—I probably would have a better idea of where I should be, or where I'd been, and when.

But I don't. Have any adult supervision, that is.

Yes, that's right. For the
first time in my life, I am completely responsible for myself.
What freedom. I am free to stuff
my face full of doughnuts at any
time. I am free to watch mindless
TV for hours on end. I am free to
cry whenever I want. In fact,
crying is the activity that seems
to take up most of my time.
Unfortunately, it also makes me
feel like a loser: pathetic,
lame, and weak. And ironically,
when I experience these emotions,
I just want to cry some more.

So that's precisely what I do.

No wonder I've always fanta-
sized about living on my own.
It's nonstop fun!

George Niven wants me to move
back in with him, back into the
brownstone on Perry Street. He
checks up on me every single
night. Of course, I'd rather spend
an eternity in hell than move back
into that house, but I keep that
to myself. I just make up excuses
about how I'm too busy to pack,

et-cetera. (That's another disturbing trend I've noticed: I've started to tell little lies all the time.) I feel too sorry for him to tell him the truth. I empathize with him. I know what he's going through. He's all alone. In fact, just thinking about him makes me want to cry again.

It's all very humorous on some level. I mean, I can be calm in a hostage situation. Put me up against some knife-wielding skinheads, and I'll be cool as a proverbial cucumber. But day to day. . . trying to fall asleep in this apartment, trying to walk to Gray's Papaya, trying to make it through a single class at school. . . I never know what I'm going to get. Tears? Rage? The sudden and desperate need to leave the room? Anything's possible.

What I wouldn't give for the days when I used to feel nothing—back when I had all my emotions folded up and packed away in a nice big steel trunk in my head.

Back when I could go through *months* without crying. Hell, there were probably two years there where I didn't feel much of anything at all. Those were the days.

But now, thanks to the many men in my life (my father, Sam, my uncle Oliver, Ed), I have no control over my feelings anymore. These men tricked me. That's what it basically comes down to. They snuck up on me, tempted me with happiness (as if such a thing actually exists), and then collectively broke my heart. It's as if they all took a secret meeting at some big hunting lodge—you know, the ones with the red walls and those huge antlers and disgusting mounted deer heads—and conspired to screw with my head: to pick the lock on my steel trunk, to drag out every single emotion I've ever had and hang it on display for the general public.

But enough about them.

Have you ever tried a doughnut shake? Neither had I until the other day. (Or was that earlier today?) Anyway, I was standing at my disgusting kitchen counter with a box of one dozen assorted Krispy Kreme doughnuts in one hand and a half gallon of milk in the other. Lunch. (Or was it dinner?) And then I saw the blender.

Three seconds later I was stuffing doughnuts down into the large Pyrex blender cup—cinnamon, jelly, chocolate glazed, Boston cream, powdered—as many as I could. Then I poured in as much milk as I could, secured the rubber lid, and slammed down every button on that blender—mix, chop, puree, *congeal,* whatever. . . I watched as all those doughnuts turned into a thick and lumpy vomit-colored sludge, and then I hurled off the lid, lifted the entire concoction to my mouth, and took a "sip."

Needless to say, it was the most horrifying dose of concentrated sugar I'd ever tasted. It was like sinking your teeth into a solid sugar cube the size of

your head. But as I spat the
sludge out into the sink full of
dishes. . . I realized. . .

That doughnut shake was a perfect metaphor for what is clearly
the true chaos of human existence.
I'm sure you see what I mean.

It's like that book we've been
reading in MacGregor's English
class. Camus's *The Stranger.*
Everything Camus wrote is dead-
on. There's no *order* to anything.
There's no *reason* for anything.
It's all just one long list of
absurd events with no payoff
whatsoever. Feel what you want;
it doesn't matter. Do what you
want; it doesn't matter.

I can't believe how much time
I've wasted thinking my life was
leading somewhere in particular,
thinking there was some kind of
master plan for me—as if there
was ever a "right" or a "wrong"
thing for me to do. There's no
meaning to any of it. We're all
just a bunch of random doughnuts,
crammed into this giant blender

for no apparent reason, chopped at, spun around, and blended together into a repulsive and utterly meaningless *mud*.

So from now on, as far as I'm concerned, the more absurd, the better. I'll just do and feel nothing and everything at the same time, in giant swirls and spins and stops and starts. No control over a stitch of it. I'll cry and then I'll be numb, and then I'll feel so unbelievably pissed off, I'll want to rip my door off its hinges and break every breakable item in this empty apartment. One hundred per- cent pure emotional free fall— total chaos in my brain. Thank you all so very much.

Control. Isn't it ridiculous? People are always trying to take control of themselves or else they're trying to control someone else. They're all so deluded. When are they going to learn? There's simply no such thing as control. None at all.

Sure, they weren't brutal rapists. But they had other faults **human** going for them. **garbage** Unreliability. Dishonesty. Cruelty.

THE SUN WAS THREATENING TO SHOW itself.

Gaia kept praying the night would last just a little longer. Somehow the days were worse than the nights. People usually complained that the opposite was true; after all, there must have been a thousand sad, lame,

Scum Exodu

cheesy songs about "lonely nights." But Gaia found the sunny days so much more depressing. All those kids screaming and laughing in the playgrounds. What the hell made them so happy that they had to scream? Was it the melting black sludge that lined the sidewalks—the last remnants of snow? Or the litter? The torn coffee cups and discarded syringes? The filth that seemed to ooze from every stinking corner of this city?

That was the problem with the days: You could see every miserable detail so clearly. Yet somehow the real garbage—the *human* garbage—managed to stay indoors.

Night was different, though. At night the scum of New York scurried out of their little holes and crevices and wrought havoc. Just like cockroaches. Turn out the lights, and they all came out to party. Turn the lights back on, and they all vanished. Judging from the deep blue of the predawn sky, Gaia had only another half hour or so before the sun came out and the scum exodus began. She still hadn't cracked any heads.

As long as there were psychos and sickos to pummel, Gaia had a hobby to occupy the meaningless and seemingly endless hours of solitude. Sleep had become a nonissue. Sleep was for the weak. Actually, she had simply been incapable of sleeping for the last few nights (four, five, six?). Which was why she was roaming Avenue D and Ninth Street at five-thirty in the morning again. Looking to kick the asses of the bad guys.

Alphabet City, as this particular area of the East Village was called, seemed to be mapped out specifically for crime. The farther down the alphabet you went, the more crime you found. Avenue B was worse than Avenue A, Avenue C was worse than Avenue B, and so on. And after midnight. . . forget about it. You might as well wear a sign saying, "Sell me drugs or mug me, please." Perfect for Gaia. *Question: What do you call a young blond girl, alone on Avenue D after midnight? Answer: Bait.*

There had already been one attempt to mug her. One very lame attempt. A guy had pushed her into a dark alley, hoping to do God knows what. Gaia hadn't even had to engage the poor idiot in combat, though; after she'd disarmed him—kicking the knife from his hands with a left jump kick—he'd taken off into the shadows. But there was usually more action—

"Get back in the car, bitch!"

Gaia swung her head around.

Not twenty feet behind her a pudgy, balding guy in one of those `neo-mafia-style jogging suits` had forced a woman in a tight red dress against the hood of a beat-up car. A flicker of adrenaline leaped through Gaia's body. *Finally,* she thought, unable to keep from smiling. It was about time.

"I don't think the date's over until I say it's over," the guy hissed.

"Stop it," the woman cried, desperately struggling to wriggle away from him. "You're drunk!"

Gaia could hear the plaintive note of fear in the woman's voice, wondering even as she broke into a sprint what it must be like to feel *afraid*. . . afraid of this ridiculously overbuffed oaf. Energy surged through her veins as she rocketed toward them. Now the guy was forcing himself on the woman, leaning into her and slobbering all over her with sloppy kisses.

"Stop it!" she shrieked, squirming. "Stop—"

"Shut up and stay still! You're just making it worse."

No, you are, Gaia retorted silently. She threw the full weight of her body against him, grabbing his shoulder with one hand, spinning, tearing him away from his victim.

"What the hell?" he shouted, eyes blazing.

His gaze locked with Gaia's. For a moment he just gaped at her, breathing hard. Then he smiled.

"Cool," he muttered. "A threesome."

This poor man. Gaia almost smiled again. He was still living under the delusion that he had control over his life—control over Gaia, control over this other woman. He still believed that he could force his will upon the world. Another hopeless sap, a sagging mountain of testosterone gone awry. Was the old cliché really true, that men were really all the same? Certainly the men in her life didn't rate much higher than Pudgy Jogging Suit here. Sure, they weren't brutal rapists. But they had other faults going for them. Unreliability. Dishonesty. Cruelty.

Kicking this guy's ass would be a pleasure. A way to take revenge upon all the slimeballs who made the world a more foul place, her father included. Yes, maybe this was her purpose in life: to teach the men of the world a lesson—that they were all swine, each in their own unique fashion.

Gaia's eyes flashed to the guy's victim. She was frozen, eyes wide, uncomprehending.

He took a step forward. "Come and get some, sweetheart," he whispered.

"Don't mind if I do," Gaia said. She grabbed his wrist, yanking him off balance. His eyes widened. Before he could react, she'd used the momentum of his fall against him, whirling and flipping him on his backside. All two hundred and fifty pounds of flesh slammed to the pavement, hitting with a smack.

"Shit!" he howled. "What the—"

A swift kick to the ribs silenced him. He writhed helplessly on the sidewalk, looking less like a human and more like some kind of animal, a giant seal, maybe. She kicked him again.

"Help!" he gasped.

Normally Gaia took the minimalist approach to a battle, just as her father had trained her. It was a lesson from the *Go Rin No Sho*: Strike only where and when necessary. Defend yourself, but do no more. Put an end to the struggle—and your opponent will think twice before he attacks again. But tonight there was another feeling creeping up on her, an added and unexpected impulse. . . one that commanded her to increase the pain, even though the competition was a joke. She had just a little less control. . .

She stared down at him in a fighting stance. She barely noticed the woman in the red dress running away down the street. The second kick definitely wasn't called for. He was terrified now, struggling to crawl away from her on all fours. Why had she given him more than necessary? He was a total nonthreat. Kid stuff. Maybe it was her new philosophy? That nothing mattered at all—that there was no sense to any of it, no point to any of it, so why not give them everything you've got? No mercy.

Maybe. . .

But the feeling ran deeper than that.

Gaia's legs began to go wobbly. It was expected, yet

another phenomenon she did not understand—utter exhaustion after a battle. Given the brief and effortless nature of this particular fight, however, Gaia was confident she could make it home without actually fainting. Yes. Already she could feel strength returning. She blinked a few times, then turned and strode down the street, back in the direction of her apartment. The sun finally began to creep up from behind the projects lining the East River—marking the official end to another sleepless night of wandering and makeshift justice.

Not surprisingly, she didn't feel any better.

"Well, we could grind our enemies into powder with a sledgehammer, but gosh, we did that last night."

—Xander

As long as there have been vampires, there has been the Slayer. One girl in all the world, to find them where they gather and to stop the spread of their evil and the swell of their numbers.

LOOK FOR A NEW TITLE EVERY MONTH!

Based on the hit TV series created by
Joss Whedon

2400-01